UNSUNG HEROES

WRITING TOURNAMENT 2022

CREATED BY W.J. KITE

WRITTEN BY YOUNG AUTHORS AGED 8-16

WT PUBLICATIONS

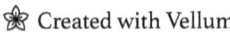

CONTENTS

FOREWORD

The Writing Tournament is quite small.

One competition in Australia offers $30 000 worth of prizes, and another in the UK attracted 100 000 young writers. When we wound up the tournament in 2021 I had ambitions to make it bigger for 2022 but as time went on, I let go of the idea because 'going big' would have meant losing what made it unique.

This year, I've written to each of the two hundred entrants to share feedback, video readings, or to ask them to read their story for our YouTube channel. One writer wrote to me to argue a case for why their main character was 'Unsung' and not 'Sung', as I'd determined. They convinced me and went on to place in the final three after almost not making the long list. Several other writers asked to form a writing group together despite being on opposite sides of the globe, needing only an email to put them in touch. We've had many lovely comments and thanks from parents and writers and, of course, been wowed by their stories. We've had emails to say the result and prizes no longer mattered, because they'd enjoyed the experience and learned from the feedback and editing notes.

Esther and Lena, last year's winners, accepted an invitation to write guest stories on any theme, and these are included in the anthology. I don't think many competitions offer such a bespoke experience to two hundred writers, so we are proud of what we've achieved these past two years.

I decided early on that I would take it year by year with the Writing Tournament and see how things went. I've chosen next year's theme so it looks likely at the moment for 2023. Let's wait and see... Until then, keep writing!

Yours sincerely,

William

PRAISE FOR THE WINNING STORIES

You are a Hero by Amelia Davis:

"This intriguing story explores the perspective of a nurse called Maddy who has never received the praise that celebrities and influencers regularly get, "You're a legend... What would we do without you?" There's no bitterness from Maddy and I enjoyed her feeling of confusion when a child finally gives her the thanks she deserves. There's some simple and effective use of language here: The "angry pink blisters", the faces of the paramedics "tight with urgency and seriousness". This is thought-provoking and timely work."
– Mark Stay

"What an interesting story! You took us into the world of a nurse - the horrors, the lack of appreciation, the challenges. I like how you gave us this introspective perspective. The child that comes into the hospital was a good choice, showing the regular tragedy that nurses have to deal with. Some great descriptive words with "angry pink blisters" being a standout for me. Well done!" – Mark Desvaux

Wilson by Phoebe Blunt

"This starts as a song to a faithful dog, the Wilson of the title, and tenderly recounts their growing up together. Then it slowly breaks your heart as you realise that Wilson is getting old, and the narrator is moving on to the next phase of their life, and not only will they not be able to spend as much time with Wilson, but Wilson's own time is coming to an end. But there's an appreciation of everything that Wilson has done, and that the time they have together is to be cherished. Lovely stuff."
- Mark Stay

"You have captured the love and companionship of a dog so well. It's a relationship someone who doesn't own a dog would struggle to fully appreciate, but you have described the very essence of that special bond.

I enjoyed how you took us through the ages, the stages as you and Wilson grew together. Descriptive words such as his "wolfish appearance" painted a vivid picture, whilst that "guardian" in his "half-sleep" gave me a sense of his protective nature.

A heartfelt account of the magic bond between you and your best friend. Very well written."
– Mark Desvaux

Hugo by Nina Basu

"Kicking off with a wonderful opening line, "Do you know what plastic bags taste of?" this is an amusing and heart-warming story of a dog that overcomes cruelty and finds strength with his pack brothers and sisters. And Hugo's faith in humans is restored by Takis, the person who rescues dogs and finds them a new home. This is quietly touching and well observed."
– Mark Stay

"Some lovely use of imaginative language here. I like the reference to 'rotten banana peel' being a step up. The smell of worry is a lovely use of the senses to connect to an emotion - brilliantly done!

You took us into the mind of a rescue animal very effectively. Well done!"
– Mark Desvaux

An Ode to the Vulture by Baker T. Beauregard

"*This grabs the reader with an inventive description of a car hitting a cat and the moment of self-preservation — "Pause (heinous)" — that drives the narrator to consider doing something terrible. I loved the grim certainty of the narrator, "Paco would not turn up... There is a criminal in each of us", and then they surprise us with flashes of tenderness. "I cried in the shower as I washed the Murder from my skin." And to cap it off the description of the business-like vultures is hilarious as it is macabre. This is a terrific read from a writer with a very strong voice.*"
– Mark Stay

"*Highly original and inventive. What really stood out was the unconventional approach and style which really grabbed my attention from the off. A dark but universal theme meant that every reader could have empathy whether they had experienced this or not. For me, the most powerful part of the piece was the analogy of the vultures as business people. This created such a great visual.*"
-Mark Desvaux

The Wheelbarrow by Saadya Lebens

"*This has a great sense of poetic rhythm as it follows a body collector through the streets of London during the bubonic plague in 1351. The author takes great delight in detailing just how disgusting the plague was (which I loved reading), but there's plenty of pathos for Hugh the body collector. A man who toils to keep the bodies from piling up in the streets, and yet is reviled by all. The cycle of death seems never ending and this is a great piece of post-Covid horror.*"
– Mark Stay

"*A good descriptive narrative which takes us in the world of a corpse carrier during the Black Death. In history class I was taught about this era, but this piece took me into the daily world of someone dealing with the horrors of death. It makes a modern day 'garbage' collector's job seem luxurious. I liked the way you showed the circle of life as one corpse carrier death became another's job. I liked how you described the contempt from others that these people experienced and made an excellent point of the valuable work they were doing. The ending was well thought out and made me wonder if Hugh himself had been carrying other corpse carriers!*"
– Mark Desvaux

The Sacrifice of Kuyili by Dharshwana Muralidharan

"*This powerful piece feels particularly timely as on the news we see women in Iran fight for their freedom. Kuyili is told that her sacrifice will never be forgotten, and she is considered by many to be the first "suicide bomber", but this story gives her a voice and heart that makes her more than just a name in the history books. This is a strong and heartfelt piece that thrills and shocks.*" - Mark Stay

"*This vivid piece encapsulates so many of the senses. It has a real authenticity to it with powerful descriptions of the palace and its surroundings. There is a wonderful change of pace when they pick up their knives, with a knowing that we are on the cusp of a dramatic scene. Writing this in the present tense and first person was a good choice and it carries the reader along. A very well written, inventive and powerful piece.*"
- Mark Desvaux

AGES 8-11 WINNERS & COMMENDED ENTRIES

1

YOU ARE A HERO

BY AMELIA DAVIS

1st Place in 8-11 age category

"You're a legend!"

"A true hero."

"What would we do without you?"

"Thank you so much for all you've done!"

"You are our hero."

"Oh, thank the Lord you're here."

"I can't imagine what we would do without your help."

I heard these words every day in my mind. Every day, without fail. As I dressed wounds, as I stitched gruesome gashes, as I closed my eyes to escape the horrors that haunted my dreams. They didn't mean much, though. It's quite different to hear it in your mind and then hear it out loud. Stitching a wound back together, they forget to say, "Thank you." Because it doesn't feel like thank you if I'm actively causing them pain.

I thought about this every day. Working in the surgery, in my bright blue nursing scrubs and matching surgical mask, I ran through the list of things people said to world influencers, leaders, celebrities. Not one of these things had ever been said to me. Not that it ought to be. Nurses just don't deserve praise.

The day it all began, when I began to wake up and grow out of my modesty cocoon, was a summery January day. Ducks were sitting on the pond, little birds were hopping onto fenceposts, a clutch of eggs was nestled into the crook of a large gumtree. It was hot, but no warmer than a usual summer's day, around 31 °C or thereabouts. I was in a pretty good mood. No surgeries since yesterday and I was enjoying a cup of coffee in the hospital kitchen.

That was when the ambulance sirens began. That wasn't unusual; it was a hospital, after all. Nevertheless, I immediately jumped up in a flash, my nurse instincts kicking in. Whenever emergencies happened, we *had* to be ready. My mask was back on, hands encased in plastic gloves and hair tied back. I was prepared for the worse.

The patient was a child, small for her eight years of age. Caught in a house fire, she was the only survivor of the family of five. Angry pink blisters covered the whole left half of her face, her wispy red hair singed. Her foot was no more, black and burned down to the bone. Fortunately, she was unconscious when she came in, otherwise her pain would be excruciating.

The paramedics wheeled her in, faces tight with urgency and seriousness, however all of them remained calm. They were well practiced at this, and it wasn't the worst injury they had witnessed. I began to help in all the ways I could, not allowing this child to pass on. The only news we had to keep us going was that the most dangerous part had passed, and the little girl was on her way to recovery.

Slowly, the number of nurses and doctors working on her decreased, until I was one of the only ones visiting her every day and changing her bandages, making sure she took her medicine, and just generally keeping her spirits up.

Her name was Elsie, and she was a lively, happy girl. Some days were better than others. Sometimes she was full of laughter, other times sombre, remembering her lost family or wincing at the pain that coursed through her body. I felt heart-burning sympathy for her, since with no living relatives left, she would have to go to foster care once she had recovered.

The only thing that surprised me every single time was when she thanked me, praised me, applauded my efforts to keep me alive. Why was she so nice? I thought. Why did she thank me for hurting her? I told this to my friends, and they laughed.

"Maddy's too modest." they said, giggling. And then they recited it, word for word.

"You're a legend!"

"A true hero."

"What would we do without you?"

"Thank you so much for all you've done."

"You are our hero."

"Oh, thank the Lord you're here."

"I can't imagine what we would do without your help."

"Maddy, you truly are an unsung hero. We love you."

2

WILSON

BY PHOEBE BLUNT

2nd Place in 8-11 age category

I need to sing this song. It's a song for Wilson, my faithful old Alsatian. He asks for so little. Soft praise, a gentle stroke and he's contented. He's always been there, his wolfish appearance strong and protective. He hasn't once lost interest and wandered away from his self-imposed duty: my guardian.

I don't remember a time when he wasn't there. Mum says that when I was a baby Wilson and I formed a special bond. The unique partnership which was forged between human and dog, based on mutual love and respect. Quite simply, we needed each other.

At night he would lie next to my cot, ears pricked and alert, listening to my steady deep sleep breathing. Remembering my sweet, warm baby scent so that he would always be able to find me. Slowly he would relax into his comfortable half-sleep that could jolt into pinpoint clarity if needed. Of course, I don't remember this time, but somehow I always knew he was there. He became familiar to me. I began to recognise him. We became members of the same pack.

When I started to toddle around the house, exploring the greater world, Wilson would be at my side. Sniffing the ground, snooping around corners, searching out any possible dangers. He never restricted my adventures, but with his steely determination he ensured I remained safe.

People would comment on his size and breed. I'd hear them criticise his intentions:

"You can't trust them."

"They're all the same."

"I've read about a vicious attack in the newspaper."

They didn't know him.

Time moved on, and my pre-school escapades, walking through the nearby woods with Mum and Wilson, widened my world. The walks were full of life, laughter, and love. Wilson would walk steadily by my side, matching my stride, as we both fell into a comfortable rhythm. The familiar thud of his heavy pads striking the ground, echoed by my tiny footfall as our walk synchronised, became a daily routine. His eager face would light up when he saw me pick up a stick to throw for him. Locked onto the swaying stick, he would anticipate my throw and bound through the undergrowth to retrieve the prize. He would swiftly return to my side to check on my safety and to deliver the treasure, which would be dropped at my feet. We loved this game. He never failed to complete the task I set for him – fetch-and-drop. He revelled in the praise that I showered upon him, the hugs and the pats and the singsong "good boy" comments. I was proud of him.

"Sit, Wilson."

"Drop, Wilson."

"Quiet, Wilson."

"Bark, Wilson."

My voice would bark out the commands, and Wilson would

oblige. I giggled at the big dog, soft as putty in my young hands. We were made for each other.

All too soon school days arrived and Wilson's walks became less frequent. Life offered different adventures and choices; my world grew larger. Wilson would follow me around as I prepared to leave for school, as if he was trying to persuade me stay – just for a while. He would lie on the kitchen floor, next to my feet, as I crunched through my toast and butter. A massive head resting on crossed paws, alert eyes drawn to my every move, my dog would watch sorrowfully, knowing that I was about to leave him. Perhaps he suspected that I was moving onto a new pack. Sensing his sorrow, I whispered into his ear that I would be home soon and we could play fetch-and-drop.

And now life has moved even further on. I have one foot in childhood and one hovering around adolescence. Wilson is still with me, my old dog. He doesn't walk much now but struggles through aching joints and unbalanced legs to follow me and protect me. He is my unsung hero. He hasn't dashed through fires to retrieve a suffocating body. Nor has he swum an ocean to drag a drowning man to the safety of the land. But I can sing this song for Wilson, my unsung hero, because he has always been in my life. As long as he breathes, I know that he would sacrifice his life for mine.

And we love each other. What more could I ask for?

HUGO

BY NINA BASU

3rd Place in 8-11 age category

Do you know what plastic bags taste of? They taste of nothing at all. Rotten banana peel is a step up. And my luckiest days as a young pup were when I found chicken entrails. Just watch out for the feathers tickling your whiskers.

The sun beat down that day. The rubbish dump was a smell banquet. I was trying to sniff out a rat.

Suddenly, my back exploded in pain. A shrill yap pierced the air. Later, I realised it had been me.

I couldn't move my legs! Then everything went black.

When I woke up, I was jolting gently back and forth. "Ah, the poor creature," said a gentle voice. "They keep dumping puppies in the rubbish." I sniffed a hand next to my nose. "Even if he can't walk again, he can have a good life," the voice continued.

"You always had a soft spot for the mutts, Takis."

"But they have no one, Iakovos."

"Don't be a fool, Takis."

Takis' courtyard was full of dogs like me. Most of them could walk and run, but some of them were like me and had to drag their legs behind them. One of them had his ears and tail cut off. Another one had a huge lump on her underside.

Takis had names for us all. He called me Hugo. It felt like an extra tail. I could never remember it. But then "Hugo!" he would call, "time for your food!" And one day, shuffling across the dirt courtyard, I thought of myself as Hugo, and then it was as much a part of me as my nose.

The woman next door used to shout at us over the fence. Early one morning, she woke up and threw a tin can at a black and white pack sister and made her squeal. Another day she emptied a bucket full of fish bones on a young pack brother who was sleeping beside the fence. The joke was on her because it was a treat! We had a grand time.

One evening after sundown a pack of neighbours came to the gate. Their vigorous banging woke us up. All of us pack brothers and sisters howled at them, but they were very loud. Their faces were red, and their brows beetled. They were led by the ferocious fishbone flinger. They stabbed the air with pointed fingers, and jabbed Takis with words I had never heard before.

"Give me thirty days," Takis kept saying. I had never seen him look so sad before. They stood around glaring. One of them spat over the gate. Then slowly, they went away.

Takis didn't sleep all night. I could smell the worry. We all could. Takis seemed smaller somehow, and paler. Every evening, he would sit in the courtyard and stare into the distance. He would be gone for ages. We never knew when he would return.

Two strange men came to our gate one day. We were ready to rush at them, but to our surprise Takis invited them in. Then they spent ages inside the house. When they came out, they spent ages poking the water pump, running their fingers across the window grills, and peering down the drains. They shook hands with Takis and left.

A few days later, Takis jangled down the road in a huge whisker-quiveringly scary thing on wheels, with a flappy back. He carried me in. Some of the others jumped in. When all of us were inside, we did a little howl to prepare ourselves. We were worried. Can you blame us?

It has been ages now that we have moved to our new home near Ierapetra. We have so much more space to run around in, and the sun shines and the breeze blows here all day. At first Takis slept in a flappy tent which blew about in the wind. And then one day, some of his friends came. They did a lot of hammering and some shouting and laughing, and grilled fish on a stick sitting around a fire, and then the next day Takis had a little room to live in, and we had little wooden rooms as well.

We sleep all afternoon, and we do our evening howl before bedtime. There are no neighbours, so no one minds. We try to share Takis' bed too, but he is sometimes a little disagreeable about muddy paws.

Even so, we are all content. It's a good life.

4
———

NEON STRING

BY VAIDEHI SANKAR

Highly Commended in 8-11 age category

Right now, you are probably sitting in a room and in that room there's probably a window. If you look outside, you will probably see many things: animals, plants, birds, and loads of others and in that mess, you might see me. I'm bigger than all the others, but I'm the most forgotten. I'm always just there, never noticed or recognised. I've gotten used to it, people adore things around me, forgetting my existence, but they always forget that without me they would never be where they are today. Now, I guess you know what I am, but for those who don't, I'm a tree.

With a 35-foot base and hundreds of branches, I'm just like the other trees. Except it's a miracle that I'm still living. It all started last summer when a few workmen came into the forest. This was a normal occurrence, as the owners of the land were doing renovations. But this visit was different. They were carrying neon-coloured strings. Now all of us trees knew what this meant. Some of us were going to get chopped. The question wasn't why, but who? Our greatest fears were coming to life, and we were going to suffer.

They walked around the forest for a while, observing us as

though waiting for us to make a move. Then it happened, they walked over to me and tied it around my waist. I didn't move a muscle; the trees couldn't show the humans that they were alive. The workmen strode out of the forest and tension rose through me. I had lived in the forest as long as I could remember and never dreamed of losing it. There was nothing I could do but accept my fate. My mind was buzzing with thoughts, most of them sorrowful, but I still had hope and never gave up. I was determined to find a way out of this situation. I looked around at my peers, they were speechless. That was understandable, what would you say to someone who is going to die in 24 hours?

I was drowning in thoughts, so I nearly didn't notice the two young girls walking up. They were only about nine or ten and one was tall while the other quite short.

"Are you sure we should do this?" the girl on the left stammered, that was when I realised they were carrying scissors.

"Do you want the trees to be cut down?" the other replied, quite annoyed.

They were going to save me. I was not going to be chopped. This made my heart leap. Maybe I was lucky. I held my breath as they circled the forest cutting the strings off the trees that had been chosen. The sun was coming down. If they weren't quick, they wouldn't get to me by sunset.

"Lilly, it's late, let's go back home," the tall one said, shivering.

"But there are still trees with strings on them, what will happen to them?"

"We can come back tomorrow morning and cut the other strings off," she replied. They didn't know the workmen were coming tomorrow morning!

The Next Morning

The sun was coming up and the workmen were arriving in thirty minutes. If the girls didn't come soon, I would suffer. I heard footsteps in the distance, I prayed it was the two girls walking up the long winding path into the forest, not burly workmen pounding their way ready to destroy. I held my breath as the footsteps became louder, then my heart dropped. The sweet girls were nowhere to be seen. I prepared myself, at least the other trees would have a happy life. Just then another pair of footsteps, lighter and bouncier than the others. It was them, they were here!

They tiptoed into the forest, ducking behind a nearby bush. We all knew that if they got caught, they wouldn't be able to finish their plan. The smallest of the pair creeped out of the bush and approached m. She pulled out a small pair of scissors and chopped the neon string off my trunk. That was it, she had saved my life in ten seconds.

We never heard from or saw the girls again, but without them, I would not be here having the time of my life writing this story.

THE LOYAL COMPANION

BY VINUDI BOGAHAPITIYA

Highly Commended in 8-11 age category

I look at him. He is walking on the footpath, in one straight line. I breathe a sigh of relief. 'He is all safe,' I say to myself, however this might change at any moment. We approach a traffic light and I stop, dead still, my eyes locked on the lights.

'Is everything alright, Barnie?' asks Bob.

Of course I can't talk, but to let him know that he is in safe hands, I reply by barking.

The red lights turn to green, so I start to walk carefully, turning my head and looking at both sides, to make sure that both Bob and I are all safe. We make our way to the footpath. I look behind to make sure that Bob is still holding onto my leash. After all, it is my responsibility to make sure that my friend is secure. I then look down to make sure that there is nothing on the ground. I suddenly spot a plastic water bottle along the footpath. If Bob steps on it, he will fall down. I stand there motionless, and Bob also stays still. I walk backwards and Bob does the same, and then I kick the bottle. We continue to walk casually until...

'Excuse me.'

I turn around to face a kind-looking roadworker. 'Sorry to trouble you, but this pathway is closed due to construction.'

I understand every word, and to let the man know I bark softly.

A smile appears on his face, as I turn around and guide Bob to the shopping mall in a different way.

As usual, we enter into the local grocery store, and everyone greets us warmly. One of the shop assistants comes to us and gives Bob a helping hand to collect our goods. After shopping at the local store, the shopping assistant calls for a taxi. We have to wait for some time and then the taxi arrives. The shop assistant helps us put our groceries into the boot, and then off the taxi goes to our home.

Unfortunately, in the middle of the road, there is a car crash. Luckily the taxi isn't involved, but we have to wait until it is safe for us to go. We arrive home safely and it is really late, about dinner time. We enter and I look at Bob, always alert and ready just in case something happens.

As Bob enters the kitchen, he walks slowly and carefully, his hands touching everything. He finds my dog food, puts it into a bowl and then hands it to me. I don't eat until Bob is ready. My eyes are focused on Bob. He is moving safely around the kitchen. He makes his way to the fridge and opens it. While rummaging everywhere he finds the salad leaves, tomato sauce and some vegetables. He then goes to a small cupboard and finds a chopping board and a knife. He carefully chops the carrot, lettuce, capsicum and tomato. Soon a fresh salad is prepared and placed on the table, while Bob toasts some beef patties. After putting the beef patties inside the burger, he makes his way to the table by touching chairs and walls.

Five minutes later, Bob is munching happily on his dinner, while I eat my dog food. We eat in silence. To let Bob know that I have finished my meal, I bark twice and he just smiles at me. When he is done, Bob goes to the bathroom to brush. I follow him quietly into the bathroom and stand there. After some time, he finishes and makes his way into his bedroom. He gets into bed and calls out to me.

'Good night, Barnie.'

I bark in reply and go to my sofa, thinking about this busy and amazing day. I think about what I did today and how well I did my duty looking after Bob. I don't need praise for my hard work, I just want to be happy and make others happy too!

AGES 8-11 LONG LISTED STORIES

KEVIN OF THE CARPARK

BY RACHEL HOUSTON

Kevin hit play on his iPod and put in his earphones. *Another great day at work*, he thought to himself happily, sitting down on a bench outside as his favourite band began playing. His job at Hillview Shopping Centre was collecting trolleys, fixing trolleys, and helping anyone who struggled to wheel their trolley. He prided himself in making sure all the trolleys were in perfect working condition. Kevin loved his job. He took it very seriously indeed. He would fix trolleys as soon as they broke and collect them into neat lines. As Kevin continued to enjoy his music, the first car of the day pulled into the carpark and parked. An old lady opened her door, stepped out, and carefully ambled to the shop entrance. She was tall and thin and was wearing an old-fashioned blue dress and carrying a black handbag. Her face was wise and calm, like an owl's. 'Hello, and welcome to Hillview!' said Kevin as the lady entered the building. The lady smiled and nodded to Kevin but said nothing. *She didn't take a trolley*, Kevin noted. *Perhaps she didn't notice them*, he thought to himself. *Or maybe she didn't need one.*

More cars pulled into the carpark. Customers came and went. Sometimes, people replaced their trolley in Kevin's neatly arranged line, but usually they just discarded them randomly throughout the carpark. As Kevin collected the discarded trolleys, he noticed a broken wheel on one of them. He was horrified and immediately took it to his repair station and gave it a new wheel. Satisfied with a job well done, Kevin lined up the trolley again with the others, and returned to his station.

The old lady from earlier in the day finally came out, carrying a couple of plastic bags. Halfway to her car, one of the bags burst open and grocery items spilled out onto the concrete in all directions. Seeing what had happened from his work bench, Kevin sprang into action, jogging over to the lady to help pick up her groceries. Arriving at the scene, Kevin noticed that a can of tomato soup was rolling away at speed down the carpark. Kevin sprinted off after the runaway can. It rolled under several parked cars, and Kevin chased it, weaving in and out between the cars. Just as he stooped down to pick it up, it hit a speed bump and went flying up into the air. Kevin was a little surprised that the can had gathered so much momentum, and reaching forward to grab the can, he tumbled to the ground without his prize. Now the can was bouncing in the direction of a shiny and very expensive looking new car. Kevin scrambled to his feet and ran like he had never run before and, diving with arms outstretched, he caught the can in his open hands just before it hit the car door.

Kevin pulled himself together and, sore from hitting the ground, he slowly walked back up to where the old lady was still standing, holding the can triumphantly in his hands.

'Thank you so much! You are the most helpful carpark attendant I have ever had the pleasure to meet!' the lady cried.

'Don't mention it.' said Kevin, panting with exhaustion and pain, yet really quite thrilled at all the excitement.

'No, really, that was extremely brave of you! You could have been hit by a car!' 'Ah,' said Kevin. 'It was nothing! I was just doing my job.'

But the lady wasn't having it. 'You're my hero!' she said emphatically.

UNSUNG HEROES

BY AYUSH PARMAR

My heart hammering like a piston in my chest, I walked through the trenches. I was in the depths of war and I had been for a long time. Engulfed in darkness, an army of overcast clouds loomed overhead as bullets of rain thundered down on my rusty cap as if joining the war. In the rat filled trenches, with bullets whistling overhead, I could faintly make out my name, 'James' on my badge below. All I could hear, smell, taste and feel were the aches and pains of the war, which seemed as if it would never end. The incessant lightning bolts were petrifying. They were like yellow knives - murdering the ash grey sky over and over again as we loaded our guns and shot at the distant enemy. Thunder boomed and rattled like a funeral drum over the dead bodies on both sides of this dreadful war. A veil of mist cloaked the outskirts of the trenches, making our vision obscure, but not as obscure as the outcome of the battle. The constant whining of bullets and screaming of bombs caused as much damage to our eardrums as the floor and terrain around it. It was horrible...

Wading through a river of corpses, I heard a horrific wailing noise. It was excruciating. I peered over to see what had happened, scared to see what I was about to witness. There was a man lying on the grass. He had been repeatedly shot. He was moaning and groaning in unbearable pain. He just lay there staring into the sky, his life slowly draining out of his ashen face and lanky legs. I ran over and lay beside him. Holding him with trembling hands, his body suddenly went limp and he stared at me, his eyes seeing something I couldn't in this cold, dark night. "It would be me next," I thought gloomily. Everywhere was miserable, wherever I looked, desperately trying to cling on to one drop of beauty and when none came, I sighed in sadness. As the bombs dropped, dust smacked our faces, taunting us and laughing at us, stinging our eyes like tiny needles but we trudged on and on, and on. The pain from the

attacking sores and scabs on our legs was overwhelming to the point I couldn't breathe, the pain wreaking havoc through my insides. Despite this I trudged on again with my fellows, through the shrieks, screams and cries of the wounded soldiers.

We were losing, and I knew it. Victory was distant. Boom! Thump, Boom! Thump. What was that sound? Trembling with anticipation, I looked round - they were all dead. Jimmy, Andy, Bob, Thomas and many others were lying on the floor with their mouths sagging help-lessly open. There were only 10 of us left now. The acrid taste of blood rose up in my mouth as a devastating fire blazed and burned, creeping closer and closer to our trench. The foul stench of the death of fallen comrades and enemies hung in the air as we fired at the enemy, the odd bullet whistling to and fro the trenches. "This makes hell look like a picnic," I thought. Every time a bomb would hit, more fire would be unleashed, their fingers spreading wildly in the dark. Sometimes, soldiers that were too close to the edge would be severely burnt and couldn't move, their skin blistered and raw. Another cry, another thump and silence for a brief moment before the bombs came back. Now it was only me. Deep in the trench, I erupted into tears, drowning in unhappiness and the blood of my companions. Death's laugh was ringing in my ears now. As the wind screamed and wailed like a banshee, all the remaining hope drained out of me like water seeping through a plug. I lay on my back, succumbing to death's clutches. Every beat of my heart seemed precious now. I clung on to them, knowing that they were numbered. Suddenly, a roar resonated around the trench. I looked around. 20,000 troops were running towards the enemy, fighting ferociously, risking their lives, while mine was becoming distant. Holding hard, metallic guns in their numb hands, they pushed the enemy back beyond the tangled maze of barbed wire. A tiny flame of hope was rekindled watching the scene. I smiled a last smile as my body fell, limp and

motionless, onto the floor, never to witness the outcome of the battle that was still strong on this dark evening.

CIRCUS LIFE

BY KAAN CORTUK

I t was yet another day of hard work and tiresome duties. I lay here, slumped in my cramped, solitary cage, my long, striped tail sweeping the dusty floor unevenly beneath my crackling body. My ears were bleeding with the raucous echo of applause elaborating from the bustling stage. Now and then, it would vibrate off the walls and thud so vigorously in my chest that it would send pain trickling through my body like ice-cold water running endlessly from a broken tap.

Each day of my disdainful circus life, I would wake up to the tumultuous clatter of my surroundings. Yet, only to be welcomed by the sharp, blinding rays of light struggling their way through a tiny hole in the roof, reminding me once again that it is my only hope for life.

Later, I am carried involuntarily by the collar and led to the stage, which would be swarming with thousands of people in just a few hours, ready to assemble for the matinee performance. As I stride prestigiously around the formidable stage, I realize that I am suddenly much more respected and appreciated- but only to be treated negligently back again in a couple of hours.

Gradually, people start filling the room and taking their places in front of the scarlet velvet curtains. As I watch despairingly friends and families laughing and cackling -and simply enjoying their lives- I cannot help but think about my worth in life. Another ordinary day, I ponder; same routine; same performance; same meal; same place. I wondered when I would ever find my freedom and meet my very own family.

Then came my turn. I slowly stepped onto the glistening, lustrous stage; there was unfathomable cheering ricocheting across the vast crowd- but I knew it would sometime end; I would return to my unnoticed life.

I had to block my eyes with my fiery-orange paws from the dazzling beams of light that shone right into my beady eyes, for I had not had a glimpse of sunlight for the last couple of months or maybe years: I had lost track of days.

Although I had performed here countless times, for a second, it felt as if the time had just juddered to a stop. As if the hands on the clock had tangled into each other. My body would not simply move. I felt like something was missing, like a piece from a jigsaw puzzle. I stood there, glued to the spot. But I knew I did not have much time: any mistake would mean another sore on my blemished skin.

"Go on..." whispered a raspy voice behind me.

Without raising alert or suspicion amongst the spectators, I turned around to see, to my great surprise, a little field mouse standing motionless behind me. The words chimed in my ears and sent vibrations to my brain, just enough for me to understand who this squeaky rodent was.

A friend.

9

THE GREAT ESCAPE

BY KATELYN TSE

The peaceful morning was greeted by the orange glow of the sun that warmed the land. The animals woke up slowly, gracefully and began their usual scurry, burrow and nestle. The quiet was soon disturbed and nothing was ever the same again.

Something angry started tearing through the landscape. Koala felt a hot rush sweep through the trees. He raced down the tree, clawing and scratching specks of bark as he crashed down. He stumbled over the sticks to escape the roaring fire behind him, as he finally got up behind a boulder, the fire mercilessly beat down his home, reducing it to just a scorched jumble of sticks and burnt food. Hours later, he was alone. Koala tried to hide a whimper but couldn't keep it in; his poor Mum. His body lay in a dark lump on the blackened earth. Moving away from the fiery storm, Koala scampered across the burnt patches of grass, feeling a sharp sting under his paws. The big black cloud swallows up more bush. Possum scampered out of the bush, coughing, escaping rings of crackling fire. A quiet cry escaped his parched lips, and his heart sank thinking of his father. Kangaroo hopped out of the smoke, black patches of burnt fur covered him, that awful smell was a cruel reminder of his family gone. He fell to the ground, hopeless, broken. Not far away Koala and Possum heard raspy breathing. Then their eyes met the helpless roo on a dark patch of grass, he was covered in mud, eyes barely open, mouth gaping and dry. Koala tugged him on the shoulder, Kangaroo opened his eyes, his eyelashes dark and crusty. His colour, sickly and legs burgundy red. Koala froze, unsure of what to say. This roo was... familiar. Even under the dry, dirty fur and buried dark eyes, Koala knew they had met before. This was the same Kangaroo that rescued his helpless bub who fell from the tree. He acted fast and caught her, buffering the blow. A different animal lay in front of her now. Finally, Kangaroo lifted his head, groaning. Possum spotted a long metal fence that had lots of volts, that separated the bush from the road. He motioned to Koala and Kangaroo with his paw.

They rejoiced. Kangaroo made his way towards the fence. Possum clambered up a striped bark tree, suddenly the memory of gliding came back to him and he hesitated in fright, backing up until his back touched the trunk, he couldn't do it. It was too long of a glide. He heard Koala and Kangaroo's heavy breathing. He saw the fire growing nearer. He closed his eyes and leapt from the tree, gliding through the air. It was Koala's turn, oh boy. He couldn't leap over the fence like Kangaroo, he couldn't glide through the air like a possum, he couldn't climb over the fence because it was volted. He heard the buzz of the electricity running through it. What could he do? The roaring fire cracked, and he knew if he wasn't over that fence he was done for. Kangaroo thought fast and grabbed Koala's arms and glided through the air but stayed in his arms and stay strong. Koala grabbed onto Possum's ankles and leapt over. Their eyes widened in delight to see Koala just miss the fence, as the fire burnt down the trees behind him. The animals were exhausted, they huddled under the skeleton of a tree, with nowhere to go. They were all each other had. As the darkness set in, the thick smoke that had clouded the air became invisible. The animals looked up to the sky and saw a grey blanket that swept across it. The world found a way to sleep, blasting noise still in their ears.

The next morning, they woke up to a scorched land. The sun shone once again, unaware of the terror known down below. The animals all huddled together; their eyes struggled against the harsh light. A large white van appeared, and three humans stepped out. Koala whispered to Kangaroo and Possum as he backed away from a large tub the humans lay down.

"DON'T GO NEAR THEM! They destroyed my home!" cried Possum.

The human hesitated before holding the suckling bottle towards Koala's mouth. With fear suspended, Koala settled down and finished the bottle in one gulp. A warm pink blanket was wrapped around their bodies to keep them warm, they turned to each other and smiled. They were safe.

10

NEKO

BY DAHLIA DUIGAN

Nestled in a corner of Tokyo's bustling Takeshita Street, among the many bright, colourful shops and stalls, lies The Cat Cafe.

Upon stepping into the feline-filled room and removing your shoes, you'll see a tree. It stands tall, presenting its branches like a model showing off her new clothes.

These branches intwined with fairy lights, wrap around the cat beds which are soft and plush

In two corners of the room, there are arched windows looking out into the street like a pair of eyes. You can sit here peacefully and play with the slinky creatures, whilst watching the busy people outside go about their day.

These very windows are where our story begins.

"MREOW!"

Mimi opened the door of The Cat Cafe and slid on her slippers. She felt a small, familiar fluffy head, rub up on her dress.

"Oh, sweet Neko, you know I visit you every day so why wouldn't I today?".

She sat down on the window seat and sighed ever so quietly. As she looked out of the window and observed the couples with their children.

She thought of her dearly departed husband and said to herself,

'Look at all those happy families having fun, how I'd like to be accompanied again'.

She blinked, quickly, a tear being hidden again behind her sweet blue eyes.

One of the cats Mimi had petted earlier, leapt onto her lap, and purred longingly. Mimi notices a little gold collar and dangling from it was a rather large round disc with the name 'Neko' engraved upon it.

'Oh, but I have all the company I need right here, don't I?', she smiled, her wrinkled hand like paper reaching forward for the kitty.

She was about to stroke the cat when the door opened with a bang. "Kitties!", a young girl says to a small baby girl.

"Have fun, okay, I'll pick you up soon", the mother reminds her, her long, jet black hair flows behind her as she shuts the door.

Once the door closes, the girl took pink slippers from her bag. One has a poorly sewn cat ear glued to the front. She noticed Mimi staring.

"I'm a pretty good seamstress, aren't I?" joked the girl. She posed and modelled the shoes as she walked over and sat opposite Mimi.

Mimi inspects the small child, a spitting image of her mother who just left, she wears a white shirt with flowers sprinkled around the collar and a faded pink skirt.

Neko the cat with a huge puff of orange and white fluff, had seen the girl and padded quietly over to her.

"He likes you too?" Mimi asked. The girl nodded and came and sat down next to Mimi.

"My name is Kichi, namae wa nandesu ka?", Kichi asked, her head tilted to one side.

"I am Mimi", the old lady replied, her face softened, and little crevices appeared at her temples as she smiled.

The two chatted together, Mimi told Kichi what all the other cats were called and told her that they had all been rescue kittens. They were lonely and needed the love of the people who came to the café.

Kichi, although not the best seamstress, taught Mimi how to sew.

Every day after that, Mimi and Kichi met at The Cat Cafe and sat together. They talked about school, cats, and baseball.

Mimi told of her home in Asakusa with its magical Sensoji Temple and Kichi told her of her home in Akasaka with its bright lights and video games.

When Mimi spoke of her life so long ago, Kichi felt different about her culture and the olden day buildings she passed on the way to school each day.

Instead of boring ruins, she imagined life inside them and thought about how much Japan had changed.

Each time Kichi told her of her life with her new video games or animae movies, Mimi felt less afraid of the outside world now. Their eras moved closer to each other as they embraced their differences.

When Mimi went home one evening, she looked out her window at the many ramen houses that lined her tiny street and smiled. Neko had brought her a new friend and she didn't feel so lonely anymore.

That very night, the bright lights of Akasaka lit up the face of a little girl who was smiling out her window too.

Across the city, Neko fell asleep, excited to meet his two best friends tomorrow.

11

THE THYLACINE TIGER

BY JAANAVHI SARAVANAN

Looking at the silent gloomy sky dropping down on the damp grass, as I breathe my last breath, I taste the air going up my mouth and down my nose. My spirit is slowly drifting away as I close my eyes knowing that I am the last one left. Darkness slowly starts to uncover through the light.

I remember my life from long ago. When I would stay in mum's pouch for about 3 months or even more – it was nice and snug there. It was amazing having my family around. Dad would tell us stories about the Palawa people of Tasmania whilst we were safe inside our den. We would sleep through the day with heavy tummies because we would hunt through the night. Kangaroos were my favourite. I had a type of snowy grey fur, while my brother and sister had more of the colour of autumn leaves.

Over time we saw more and more humans entering our territory, but these ones were different to the Palawa. They had fair skin. At first, we did not mind keeping out of their way, and they kept out of ours. Until the day they felt we were suddenly in their way and started to cull us. Losing respect for our pack.

It only seemed like yesterday my brothers and sisters were here with me, but now they are all gone. Dingos and hunters came, they attacked us from the bushes, and we had no time to strike. I was the only one left that day. It was one of the saddest moments of my life.

I surrendered to the hard earth one last time knowing I was alone in the dark. For the last time I lay my head on the damp grass, suddenly feeling my eyes closing in the gloomy midnight sky. I knew this was my last day. Extinction was here for us.

12

THE BEACH THEY CALLED GALLIPOLI

BY ARABELLA HOPE

The boats took us onwards,
Into the land of the unknown
The waves crashed unforgivingly,
Forward, we were thrown.
The men around me vomited,
And fear was making my world spin,
The air around me seemed to evaporate and thin.
We scattered, scrambled, tumbled,
Through the water,
Onto the beach,
But safety seemed to dance away,
Just metres from our reach.
The lads beside me dove for the sand,
But land mines were buried well,
Their severed limbs flew in the air,
And landed in the swell.
My mates cried out in pain,
And gunshots echoed loudly,
This beach will never be the same,
I hope their souls rest soundly.

War has no winner,
It never truly ends,
I am proud of our country, the country I defend.
Poppies will spring up,
Where our bodies lie,
And for those who fight for liberty,
They shall never die.
And as the sun sets,
On the damage we have done,
Pray they let us all forget,
The war no country won.

I YELLED in agony as my arm was hit,
Blood ran down my arm,
I tried to stop the flow with my ever-shaking palm.
A crack, A bang, A smack, A clang,
My helmet hit the ground.
I looked across at the sea,
And died
On the beach they called Gallipoli

13

NEW BEGINNINGS

BY ELIZABETH EATS

'Monday mornings are so annoying,' I mutter to myself quietly. I let myself sleep a little while longer. After a short period of time, I heave my way out of bed and pull off my p-j's. I find my school clothes and put them on. I take a moment to breathe, and I see the sticker of an 8 on my wall symbolizing my age. My feet shuffle to the kitchen as my mum calls to me from the dining room.

'Hey there, Princess Georgia, breakfast is ready.'

'Coming and don't call me princess,' I reply to my mum Maya jokingly. I scoff down breakfast and pack my bag for school.

'To the bus we go,' I yell to mum

WHEN WE ARRIVE at the bus-stop, my friend Angela is waiting for me at the back of the bus. 'Angela!' I shout as I run up to her. I sit down and talk to Angela about how this is the last Monday of term one. We got to school, and I made my way to my table. Class started with maths, my favourite subject.

· · ·

WHEN WE WENT out to recess Angela's little sister Millie came up to Angela and I, asking if we could help her find her hat that she lost. Of course, we said yes. I looked all around the school. It turned out the hat was stuck in a tree, so I had to climb the tree and get it. The bell chimed for recess ending. Since it was the last Monday of term one, we played games all through to the middle of the day to lunch.

ANGELA and I were talking about term two, we're all so excited. We ate our salad sandwiches our mums had packed, then went off to play on the playground. What felt like five minutes of playing was one hour of playing. When we arrived inside, Mrs Grace's smile was wider than ever.

'Listen up everybody! I just got off the phone with the principal and...' she trails off and the class erupts into a chorus of sighs and groans. 'It's not a test guys, settle down! As I was saying, we have a new student coming next term.' Whispers ripple through the kids. 'We will be coming up with some awesome ideas to make her feel welcome.' I can hear students brainstorming. 'Her name is Madeline, she's very shy, so we need to make an extra special effort.'

FIVE MINUTES later I walk into my house greeted by mum and Billy my French bulldog. I tell mum all about my day and about Madeline. The next day I do my daily routine of getting ready for school and jump onto the bus. 'Have a great day, honey,' mum yells before the bus door closes.

I BLOW her a kiss and smile at her. At school we had discuss where Madeline will sit. Miss Grace says she can sit near me. 'I know what will make her feel welcome, we could have a welcome party at the town hall,' Angela suggests.

.   .   .

'GREAT IDEA, I WILL ORGANISE IT,' Miss Grace exclaims. I can't wait for the party. The rest of the week goes fast and now it is the holidays. On the first day of holidays, Mum gets a message from Miss Grace saying, 'Next week there will be a welcome party for Madeline.'

'We should make biscuits,' Mum suggests. 'Let's get to it,' I command.

We chose to make one batch of chocolate biscuits.

THE NEXT DAY we get up and start making goodies for Madeline and her family. We do not have enough sugar from our cake but Jason our neighbour lends us some.

WE HAD MADE ALL the goodies in time for the party. We drove to the town hall early to introduce ourselves to Madeline.

'Hi, I'm Georgia, one of your new classmates.' I say as I approach Madeline.

'Hi 'she replies.

'I hope you like this town,' I say more confidently.

'I do like it. I want a...' Madeline paused, fiddling with her hands. 'A friend' Madeline stumbles

'Easy fix, c'mon I'll introduce you to everyone.' I smile and take her hand.

14

VISIBLY INVISIBLE

BY REBECCA LI

T he ants scurried in an odd symphony, coordinated, yes, but yet it was strangely chaotic, chaotically organised and unpredictable. To the human eye, they looked like long cylindrical black dots hurrying around as they disappeared into their deep cosy abyss. And that was it, that was what we could see. Behind, it was different. It was a thousand armed soldiers in black suits entering a foreign, unbelievably dangerous land to find resources for the colony to survive. Very little are successful, most souls being reaped under the revolting human. However, some are lucky.

On the pavement, an ant spots a simple brown roach carcase.

She saw his bloodshot eyes, the veiny red engulfing his murky white eyeball, his bright blue pupil no longer the centre of beautiful euphoria, but rather hid something that made her want to crawl into a corner and never come out. *How?* How did the beam of light become the centre of darkness? She kept her eyes on him during class as he slumped forward in his chair. He was barely holding on, as if there was something deeper, as if something had a hellish grasp on his mind that he couldn't ignore. Even his classmates had begun to question his lack of enthusiasm and his empty contagious smile, but they had kept quiet.

"Alright everyone, that's recess. Don't forget the history project due next week," she announced over the bell.

Her students suddenly became a blur of bodies as they hurriedly squeezed themselves through the door, but through the chaos, she had managed to find the distinct figure. He held his head low, like something was dwelling on his leg and was sluggishly engulfing him into the indefinite abyss below.

"Hey, could you stay behind?"

She stared at the hooded figure, his brows furrowing over his eyes as his hair was buried deep into his hoodie, highlighting the intense dark rings that beamed under his puffy eyes.

"If you need an extension or some help with the assignment, I'd be happy to give it," her voice was soothingly gentle. But then she looked into his eyes, and she had seen it all.

"Hey, is everything okay at home?"

His eyes widened as he tucked himself in.

"It's okay, you can tell me," she embraced his hands into her palm as her warmth filled his body.

"She-," he swallowed back his tears that had already started glistening from the corner of his eyes. "She's been doing it tough. I-I've been working to help with the costs. I hate seeing her like this. I hate it all. It hurts so muc-"

Then it came tumbling down, all of it, all the hidden sadness he'd kept back that he didn't know he had kept secret, all of the sadness he'd swore to never let out again, to never wound his scarred body. There was so, so much. The classroom was only filled with the crushed cries of someone who had kept it in so, so deep. But then it came out, and it had broken everything.

***

She didn't know how many hours she'd been there for, but

however long it had been, helping a, *her* student that she'd seen grow and be so brave, was worth whatever.

"Listen to me," she squeezed both his shoulders. "You and your mum are going to be okay. You have been so brave and strong so far but now, I'll help you. I can help your mum find a job. I'll make sure you'll never have to worry about that stuff again. It'll be okay. I'm with you this time."

She wrapped her arms around him as he could feel himself at ease. He had someone now, someone to share this burden with, someone who had the ability to take this burden away.

"Thank you. Thank you so, so much."

When everyone else had given up, when everyone else had chosen to ignore, she hadn't. It doesn't appear on her resume, doesn't get recognised by anyone, but it made a difference, a big one. She had helped someone; she had helped Jonathan.

By then, the carcase had disappeared down into the deep cosy abyss of the ant hole. On the pavement, an ant spots a simple brown spider carcase. It quickly snatches it before a five-year-old walks past and freaks out. It was gone within a second, the pathway clear for any wandering giants.

Our little cleaners.

15

SPIRIT WEEK

BY JOSEPHINE

M onday: Dress up like your favourite animal…"
I was so excited that I stopped reading right there. My favourite animal is a tiger, and I had the perfect tiger costume in my closet, all orange and black stripes and a tail, and a hood with ears that stuck up. I ran upstairs to my bedroom and slid open the closet door. The costume was there, but not where I expected it to be. Instead, it was crumpled in a ball on the floor.

Darn it! I thought. I didn't know how to use the laundry machine. Normally, I would ask mom to help, but she was busy with my little sister.

Once, when she was taking care of Anna, I asked her if we could go to the store to get a new robot toy that had just been released. But my mom explained that she was too busy because she needed to cook and put my little sister to bed. I was mad: all my friends had gotten one, and I wanted my own really, really badly. That day, I stormed off to my room and slammed the door.

But that was the past. Now, I knew better. I could take care of things myself.

I took the costume downstairs to the laundry room and put it in the machine. "How hard could it be?" I asked myself. An hour later, I went back to check on the wash, and when I looked at my costume it had completely shrunk! It was so small that my little sister would be able to fit in it.

I didn't have another tiger costume, so I knew I needed to do something. I tried stretching it out, but it only got a little bigger. Upset, I closed the laundry machine and took the costume to the living room, where I tried to stretch it out again.

It was hopeless.

After my mom put Anna to sleep, I showed her the costume and told her what had happened. She said that it was time for me to go to bed. I was angry: she was so busy taking care of Anna that she had forgotten about me. Now it was too late to do anything. On Monday, everyone else at school was going to be dressed up in their costumes, and I was going to have to wear regular clothes.

The next morning, I woke up late. When I went downstairs, I saw my mom walking in the front door holding a bag. I asked her where she was, and she surprised me by saying that she had bought me a new costume. When she handed me the bag, I took the costume out and ran up to my bedroom to try

it on. While I was changing, I started thinking about how nice she was. "Maybe she doesn't give me a lot of attention sometimes," I thought, "because she's taking care of Anna all the time. After all, Anna's a baby, and can't do anything for herself." I started to realize that this is how my older brother felt when I was younger.

I looked at myself in the mirror. I looked all around the tiger costume and tried on the ears that came with it. I even imagined myself being a tiger, hunting in a rainforest with different animals and walking around in the tall bushes, looking for a deer to eat.

I loved it.

16

MY CHRISTMAS LIGHTS

BY BALLY NAPTHALI

When I was a little boy, my parents showed me how to love
They taught me that through special moments, people go above
At certain times of the year, our eyes are more awoken
We realise our circumstances aren't all the same and many feel quite broken
When I was a tender two years old, my first experience stuck
I released that the surrounding world wasn't made from luck
I saw the suffering, I felt it too and realised it was sad
All the years, and so many days passed and all I'd felt was glad
That at the age of two, I hadn't lived what others had endured
Concepts so foreign in my home that thoughts quickly conjured
At two, so many knew the pain of going without a meal
Of rarely having parents' love that could subconsciously heal
The visible wounds, the hidden hurts, the hunger and the wanting
All things that a child like me was never fully contemplating
For I was busy eating snacks, and being cuddled when I cried
The soul inside me realised I was a privileged little child.

. . .

It was at Christmas time, when my parents were outside

Spending hours upon hours, no longer the sole focus of their pride

I asked them what they were doing and their answer I felt deep

Honey, they said, we are bringing joy to people's outlooks that are bleak

Life isn't simple, and at certain times, many often feel deep sorrow

But what we do each year is show a brighter chance for tomorrow

Many people can't buy food, presents or even power

But our Christmas lights bring people together where they can then shower

The people who need it most with love, and food, money, even smiles

A connection, an opportunity, a chance encounter travels many miles

I wish I could say that these lights are all just for Christmas cheer

But the reality is that they mean so much more when people start to hear

The suffering, the help, the needs, the connection

Poverty isn't one dimension

Humans have necessities and if we can provide even a small amount then we should

Because life is different to what you just see and even a small child like you could

Make a difference when you just smile and lend your parents for an hour or few

You are giving what you can even at the tender age of two

My parents then thanked me for letting them have this precious moment,

To create a magical journey that brings a great bestowment

Where Christmas lights bring joy to many normal faces

But the true joy comes from helping those who live in difficult places

The joy, the sorrow, we all unite, to help each other at this time

For there's no better journey than the one where you help a person that isn't fine.

17

HERO IN DISGUISE

BY ABIGAIL LEE

Five hundred and fifty teachers and students are at my school. There are various helpers, but one is taken most for granted. The janitor, Mr. Luiso. He does the jobs that other people wouldn't want to do at all, and he does more by making friends with the students. He does his job with a constant smile on his face.

Imagine this-

You get up at 5:30 while everyone else is asleep and start off by cleaning the halls of the six grades in the school briefly. You then fold up the tables in the dim-lit school cafeteria in order to prepare for the young's P.E. class. A single line of light turns on, signifying that more council has walked in. You take a breath in, put a smile on your face, and get ready for an eventful day at work.

All lights turn on, and hundreds of children running and talking fill the halls. Kids running up, saying hi, and staff just passing. Every half an hour the halls go from chaotic to dead silent, as you run around trying to clean tables, fold them up and down, communicate with staff, and stack chairs. Midway doing so, you go on a lunch break.

Usually that would mean this:

Don't text me, don't call me, don't talk to me.

But in this scenario, you are open to everything, and most likely will have to pause that lunch break to lift heavy furniture and help teachers with mundane tasks. People rarely say thank you, just "see you around, Mr. Luiso!" Your hard work is something people are used to and take for granted. It's not your job to be nice to kids or interact with them, you don't get paid to be a friend. You do it for the sake and pleasure of purely the children. As you pass, people nod their heads and keep walking.

As you repeat the morning's process over three hours total left, except cleaning everywhere, you notice thank you cards to the nurse, the principals, and teachers. Why not us, too? Because in most people's brains they think- "Why thank a janitor?" This is why.

People get used to having a friendly janitor for advice and help when regularly the janitor isn't required to do this. It's a personal choice. A personal choice that will break you. You painstakingly stay an hour or two after school hours are over. You love being there for kids, but is there anything in it for you other than the realization of how people take you for granted?

Congrats, you've made it through a day in Mr. Luiso's shoes.

When all's said and done, it's true that doctors and nurses are heroes, but the unnoticed- everyday heroes always come back to people like Mr. Luiso.

18

THE POWER OF MAMA

BY ADRIAN HUANG

Once there was a poor family. The dad was always working for money. Every day at home, the mom was always doing laundry, washing dishes, cleaning the house, taking out the trash, making food, and more. The child always thought the mom was useless because she did not make any money for the family. The child always said disrespectful words about the mom and about how she did not do any work. The father was also making fun of the mom because she was not doing any work.

One day, the mom got tired of it and said, "How about I take a break for one week and see what would happen?" The father and child agreed. The first day was going fine. He had clothes to wear and food to eat. The house was all clean and fresh. The child thought, "What could possibly go wrong?" He was incorrect. The next day was awful.

The next day, the child ate leftovers for breakfast. When he went to change, he realized that he was running out of clothes and the dirty clothes basket was full. He still thought it was okay. When he went to the kitchen, the sink was full of dishes and smelly trash. He was about to call his mom to do it, but he remembered she was taking a break. Then he thought, "It's not that bad; I can do it myself." He started doing the dishes. By the time he was done, his arms were sore from all the scrubbing. Then he had to take out the trash. He was super tired by the time he was finished.

When the child woke up, he went to change clothes, and he realized that he did not have any more clean clothes! He saw the basket of dirty clothes and sighed. He went to do the laundry. He had to move all the clothes to a specific area and had to clean all of them. Then he had to dry them. He moved them outside and hung them up. It took him one hour to accomplish his task, and it was super tiring. He went inside and went to get food, but there wasn't any. Now he had to make his food. It took another 30 minutes to get his food ready. He was so tired. His dad did not help, so he was alone.

When he was finished eating, he went to sit on the couch and realized that the house was super dusty, and the floor had dirt on it. He went to get a broom and started to clean the

floor. Afterwards, he had to clean off all the dust. Finally, he was done with the chores; he laid on the couch and watched TV. He was so tired that he fell asleep on the couch.

The next day he woke up on the couch. He went to make breakfast for himself, and afterwards, he went to take the dried clothes inside. He had to fold all the clothes and put them back into all the drawers. He was so tired and regretted saying that his mom was useless. The rest of the week was basically this routine every day.

On the last day, his mom spoke to the child and the father about their week. The child said he was sorry for saying that she was useless, and the father said, "I am starving; can you make me some lunch?" The mom was super angry that they both thought that she was useless. She asked, "Do you finally understand how hard it is to do everything inside the house?" The dad and child nodded. They both learned a lesson that a mother is very hardworking and should be appreciated. Moms are truly 'unsung heroes.'

19

MY TEACHER

BY JORDI NGUYEN

Lots of people think that heroes are people who can do big things like rescuing other people. But to me, a kid who has just turned eight, heroes are people that are always helping people the best they can and are dedicated to what they do. Furthermore, some heroes are people who don't need and never ask to be paid back. Those people are called unsung heroes. Therefore, my unsung hero is my teacher - Mr. Conneally.

My teacher is a teacher who has given me the best he can. I can still remember the first time I asked him if I could borrow a book to take home. The very next day, he gave me two books which suited my level. Also, my teacher gives me lots of thoughtful advice which helps me in learning and in life. When I send him my work, he always replies in a short time with not only compliments but different ways to try to improve me. My teacher knows my learning level very well. He knows my strengths very clearly, so he gives me extra work to develop my skills. The things my teacher does for me are not only for learning but also for my life. My teacher helps me be a better version of myself. However, the thing that makes me most emotional is that everything he does for me he does for the rest of the class, although there are 28 people in the class. Not every single teacher can do the things my teacher does for me and my class. I am very proud to be my teacher's student.

My teacher does everything in a happy way. With 28 people in the class, there are 28 different personalities. Sometimes the class is good, sometimes they might be the opposite and don't listen to him. But, no matter how the class is, my teacher is always patient with the class. I have never seen my teacher shout. "Monkeys see, monkeys do. Children see, children do.". Because my teacher is happy and patient the class will grow up and be like him.

So, how is my teacher an unsung hero?

No one knows about the amazing things my teacher does for the class. Only the students in the class know about the great things he does. He does the great things quietly, and not so that he can get paid back from the students or the parents. What he does is spend more time than expected. He isn't forced to do the things he does. He does it because he loves his job and the class. The silent way that he does everything for the students and the parents makes him my unsung hero.

"A teacher takes a hand, opens a mind and touches a heart.". My teacher is definitely a teacher who takes my hand, opens my mind and touches my heart. My teacher is not only my teacher, but he is also my mentor. I wish all teachers were like my teacher.

An unsung hero can change your life completely.

20

THE POWER OF FUNGI

BY YACHEN HUANG

What was the first thing that made medicine–the first origins of antibiotics–? People might say that Alexander Fleming created the first antibiotics, but that is wrong. It is actually just a group of bacteria and fungi in an arms race against each other. These bacteria and fungi have developed chemical weapons that kill the other species. These chemical weapons, especially from the fungi, were turned into the antibiotics that we know today, so why did these microbial creatures decide to fight each other, and what makes these fungi special enough to produce their own "antibiotics"?

These fungi developed these countermeasures because bacteria would often steal their resources that they needed. These fungi cannot afford for bacteria to steal their well-earned resources. Think about it: would it be helpful if a certain species keeps on stealing resources that the species needs desperately? Since the bacteria keeps on stealing the fungi's resources, these fungi produce penicillin to fight the bacteria by basically destroying their cell walls. The penicillin binds to the important molecules in the cell wall and does not allow the cell wall to repair itself. It also destroys the cell wall which just kills the bacteria altogether. This makes that one fungus incredibly effective in killing bacteria with this approach. The thing is it did not just kill one type of bacteria; it is very effective against many types of bacteria since most bacteria that have not been fighting against the fungus do not have a way to counter this. This makes this fungus very useful for treating infections.

This is one of if not the most important discoveries ever made in medicine. This discovery cannot be understated. Humans have been battling various diseases, which range from smallpox to COVID. These diseases killed lots of people and caused mayhem when the disease became prominent, so this discovery cannot be understated. Due to this discovery, humans could fight some of the deadliest diseases better. This fungus is useful since most of the deaths at the time were from diseases like cholera and other types of bacteria.

Despite the usefulness of this fungus, it is not very well known. This discovery saved the lives of many people who would have died from common infections such as tetanus and tuberculosis. Before penicillin was used for medicine, these bacteria were common and ravaging the world and killing millions. Penicillin helped cure or at least helped the people with those diseases. This is HUGE, especially since this natural cure has existed for a long time. This fungus would change the course of medicine itself. By having a cure to most bacteria, the world's population slowly grew to the current size it is today.

This incredible fungus has changed the modern world. It has shaped the world by making diseases easier to fight, and starting an entire study is such a big accomplishment, especially when the fungi was just the size of a couple micrometres. This microbe, despite being very small, saved the lives of so many people! Most people would not think that a small fungus could do that. This is why I think this small creature is an unsung hero.

21

WORMS: THE REMARKABLE, REGENERATING, AND REPRODUCING, UNSUNG HERO!

BY QUENTIN LENNOX

In our world, there are lots of people and animals that don't get praised or noticed for their hard work, courage, or great achievement. Out of all of these people and animals, the worm is the ultimate unsung hero. There are many reasons why worms are underappreciated despite their many capabilities. We normally react by killing worms whenever we see one; this causes disbelief about how worms are useful.

In this world worms are underappreciated for many reasons. Generally, though, this is due to humanity's perceptions rather than science and actual fact. One reason why they are not appreciated is that they are perceived to be disgusting. Because we see them as creatures that wriggle in the ground, we have the normal human instinct to kill it. Another reason why they are uncredited is because people *think* they are useless and do not contribute to anything (even though this is not true). Many people think worms are useless because they are small, pink, and unintelligent and normally out of sight and, therefore, unnoticed. They are deemed insignificant with no real value as a result of their small appearance and seeming unintelligence. Because we see them as disgusting, "useless," and insignificant creatures, we undervalue them and do not bother to notice their skills and actions that help us.

Worms have many abilities that go unnoticed that should far outweigh this natural instinct, however. One ability worms have is being able to decompose objects like dead bodies and dead plants. Without the rotting carcasses that could fill the planet, plants are able

to grow. Another reason why worms should be appreciated is that they create fertile soil by breaking down dead carcasses. Decomposition along with fertile soil allows nature to shine through. As a result of the conditions that worms create, plants thrive. Worms are also a very important food source for the animals that eat them (such as the mealworm and the domestic silk moth). They have proven their worth with their two parts in the food chain: decomposers and prey. Worms are useful and important to our environment ("Why Are Worms Important?").

A last important ability they have was shown to me through an experiment my brother held last year with worms. He tested the worm's capabilities with full-body regeneration' and nerves (and also the impact of chemicals on them). Worms could continue to live and move even when cut into pieces, which is amazing. Their survival abilities despite their small body was also such. It also taught me how important and valuable worms are to help further research in science. Scientists could use that information to figure out how to use regeneration on humans. In all, I learned the regeneration of worms and how they can be useful to scientists rather than just nature.

An unsung hero of our world is the worm. They are helpful and important and should, therefore, be better appreciated and noticed because of their small but greatly impactful actions.

WORKS CITED

"Why Are Worms Important?" *Soil Association*, https://www. soilassociation.org/causes-campaigns/save-our-soil/meet-the- unsung-heroes-   looking   -after-our-soil/why-are-worms-impor-

22

WHO IS THIS UNSUNG HERO?

BY LINYI HUANG

There is a photo: a sunshine filled man; his smile as nice as a flower. He hugged a little girl beside him. This photo was taken at Adelaide Show. It was a gorgeous day. A nice and bright sun shone along with clouds like cotton candy making the sky beautiful.

They originally lived at an also quite nice city in another country. One day, the man decided that he wanted his family to live a better life. Every day after he came back from work, he searched lots and lots of resources. Fortunately, it didn't take a long time until he found his opportunity. He passed the interview online smoothly.

Before he went overseas there was an important thing he needed to achieve. That was a 6 grade in the IELTS test. But to him, it's very hard because English was his second language especially oral English as he hadn't had much chance to communicate with English speaking people. To make matters worse, he only had two months before the departure. He tried hard to get ready and then he made the first attempt. Not surprisingly, he failed on his speaking at 5.5 points. He was almost there, just 0.5 points to pass. He picked up his mind quickly and practiced for another month then went to the test again. This time, he got 6 on speaking, but on writing he only got 5.5

points. It was a very upset result because he had got no time to do another test.

At the end of that year. The man started his oversea journey alone. Due to there was heaps of uncertain. He kept his wife and daughter at home. Then he started to settle into a totally new world---new friends; new job; new culture; different language and even the different foods. More importantly, he used all his spare time to prepare another IELS test. This time he separated his spare time into four groups: for writing, he wrote an essay every day. For listening he watched movies and T.V. news in English. He pushed himself to talked to the colleagues in the company as much as possible even though they didn't understand him at the beginning. Because he was good at reading comprehension, he didn't use much time to prepare it. 3 months later, he went again confidently and thought he could pass. But... he was defeated again!

What would you do if you were in that situation? Would you give up? Most people would give up and not have any confidence to go again. However, when he looked at the

photo and thought about his daughter, he encouraged himself again. He was positive and full of energy to keep going and going. On his eleventh tries, he finally made it. He felt great and very happy. Not long after, he was able to stay and live permanently. After that he could eventually reunion with his small family -- the beloved daughter and wife.

Can you guess who the man in the photo is? That's right---he is my lovely dad. In the dictionary, a hero means a man or boy who has done something very brave. To the rest of the world, my dad is nobody, just a man. But to me, he is my hero. He bought a house and gave us a sweet home in Australia. He made me experience a new culture. And he is hard working, brave, nice and lastly a hero to the whole family.

23

THE HERO IN MY EYES

BY FAYE ANAGNOSTOPOULOU

Lately, my parents told me I'm like a hissing kettle, full of angry bubbles all the time. I think it's because I don't spend much time with Aris as I'm at school and he's at nursery.

Aris is my little brother and a true hero in my eyes.

When I'm facing a problem or feeling upset, Aris will not register that fact. Instead, he would become even more upbeat and start giggling or laughing at the top of his voice. I found this annoying and sometimes infuriating, but I often burst into laughter with him at the end. I may argue with him, and we would make up. I may still be grumpy, but he would become shamelessly happy and sometimes even start singing. I just have to get over what has happened and carry on.

Aris teaches me many different life lessons, such as patience being important. One of the things I learned is that we must move on after an argument. He does not say this but explains it with action. It may not be apparent this is what he is doing. He himself may not know, but he really is doing it in a truly extraordinary way.

There are other examples. I often whisper in front of other people, even my family. They would say, "please can you talk at normal volume? We can't hear you!" Sometimes, I can't speak out loud because I don't know how to say things. My mind went blank, and the words didn't come to me. Sometimes, I don't agree with what other people have said but don't want to tell them. I would speak quietly, thinking I just wanted the conversation to end. Aris is not like this. When he is talking, he talks very loudly and often won't stop for minutes, even if he is told to. He taught me that people listen to him because they know what he is thinking. People don't understand me because they simply can't hear.

Other times, I talk to him, and he ignores me completely as if he cannot hear me. He might start playing or speak to my parents. He doesn't just do this to me but also to others. I guess a person can be selective with what they want to hear. You don't have to be interested in everything other people say.

All of these can be extremely frustrating when I am at the receiving end. The interactions with him test my patience. These situations are practice for keeping my temper under control.

He also does something that I have not seen others do. He would start singing for no reason that we could observe. He would keep singing with made-up melody and lyrics. He would sing and sing and eventually make sounds because there were no more words to use. These random songs show that you just have to keep at it. When you are happy, you have many different ways to show it.

Aris taught me many things. I have become patient, annoyed, cheerful, angry, happy, jealous, cheeky, tired, and sometimes worried since he was born, but never bored. It is always a mix of many feelings, especially during the lockdown year when we spent much time together. I miss spending time with him for all the arguments and plays. But soon this will change, he is entering the reception and is going to my school after Summer. We will see each other more often, even if it's not the whole day.

He may be naughty in the eyes of others. People do not take notice of the lessons he taught me, but they are truly important. He is my unsung hero.

24

MY MOTHER

BY LIAM NOUWS

I am going to talk about my mother (she is Japanese), the most courageous hardworking person I admire. In Japan, my mother had a job as a travel agent and tour guide. My mother had enough of her job and left Japan and went to Australia to learn English and get a job. When the plane landed in Australia, travelled to Noosa. She stayed and worked in Noosa and met my father one week later. She went back to Japan then came back to Australia as she was not happy there. After she came back, she made friends with Rick and Shel, the people living across the road from where she was renting a room from a friend. (That friend ended up being my father). My mother worked hard learning English and studying accountancy at university until she had to go home to Japan when her visa expired. She didn't have enough money to extend the visa. She lived in Tokyo for one year.

My father was very lonely by himself after my mother went home. He went across the street and asked Rick and Shel what he should do about his loneliness. Shel told him to hop on a plane and ask my mother to come back to Australia with him. So, like Shel said, he caught a plane to Japan and asked my mother to come back with him. Then, he asked Baba (My grandmother) and Jiji (My grandfather) if he could marry their daughter. They said yes and he brought my mother back to Australia. When they got back to Australia, my mother and father married. There was no work in Noosa so my mother decided to study accountancy. She sat an English exam and passed on her first try. During the same year, my sister and I (We are twins) were born. While looking after my sister and I, my mother did another three things every day. She started her studies for university again, taught herself English and kept the house in order. While she was studying, my sister and I were not in the house as we were at kindergarten, that left her time to study.

My mother graduated from university with High Distinctions. She got a job as an accountant. After she graduated, my mother took my sister and I to Japan to visit Baba and Jiji. Sadly, my dad didn't come because he had to look after our dog and keep working.

Now, my mother is working full time and studying for CPA. She still has a job as an accountant.

COURAGE: My mother had the courage to come to Australia three times by herself.

HARD WORKING: She is very hard working because she was able to run a house, look after two naughty children and study for her exams at the same time.

ACHIEVEMENTS: Her achievements are that she passed her English exam first try, taught herself English with only a tiny bit of help from some people she knows, graduated from university with High Distinctions, got the job she studied for and now studying for CPA.

My mother looks after my sister and I well, teaches my sister and I the stuff that school doesn't teach us and works very hard for her job.

25

A LIFE FOR ANOTHER

BY RUIXI XU

Nurses are just like doctors. They help and interact with our daily lives. Nurses help with medication, or health check-ups, but I had ICU nurses. They helped and guided me and many others through COVID. It affected my dad and I terribly, making us suffer, feeling like we were a step away from dying. My favourite nurse in the unit was Linda and she was very lovely. A charming woman my dad forenamed. Linda was very kind to me and always made me happy even when I was feeling the worst. There were also other ICU nurses like Mr Robertson, who was very funny and entertaining.

THE NEXT TWO days I lied in bed wondering when I could leave. It seemed like the world had changed once I became trapped in a hospital. My friends were gone, and my family could not see us very often either. The only way I could see the world again was through the news, which only updated me on the daily stock market; something I was not interested in. I spent the rest of my afternoon looking outside and listening to the BP monitor's continuous beeps. I also made a friend, called Daniel. He's allowed to leave the unit tomorrow and quarantine at home, but definitely not me. Lucky him, I know. Linda came in and interrupted my daze to check how I was doing.

"I might not be able to come for one or two days because I have to go get a Covid test," Linda said to me.

"Ok, you will come back though, right?"

Linda smiled. "Maybe." I heaved a sigh and sat there on my bed. I thought about how much Linda had done for me. *How much does she get paid for this? Maybe she's wealthy! Or perhaps just a normal person.* I broke out of my thoughts and glanced at the clock. It was nine o'clock so I tried to get some sleep.

THE NEXT MORNING when I woke up Mr Robertson was standing by my bed.

"Aghhhhh!" I checked the clock and it was only eight in the morning. "What are you doing staring at me? It's only eight o'clock! I could've slept for another hour or two!"

"Well at least you get to sleep, we have to stay up all night just in case one of you people start dying. Anyway, I am here to inform you that Linda is very sick and will not attend work for a while," Mr Robertson said.

"So...she got Covid?"

"Yes."

I looked out the window, sun reflecting onto my face. Sadness flowed around my body.

"It happens to a lot of us, and most people don't really care so there is no need to worry," Mr Robertson assured. Now more people have disappeared from my side. Daniel went home and Linda was gone too. I felt bad. I'm sure it was because of me that Linda got Covid. She had worked so hard and had still gotten sick.

MR ROBERTSON CAME to visit me again during lunch to take a test. He came back with the results after and said I would have to stay in the unit for another week and a half. That made me feel a bit better knowing that I could live freely and not be trapped in a room. He left just as lunch came. It was meatballs and mashed potatoes, and it tasted terrible and rubbery. *I would've enjoyed it more if Linda was here* I thought.

A WEEK PASSED and I woke up to hear a voice saying, "Sorry darling, are you awake yet?" It was my Dad shaking my shoulder, while trying to explain something. "It's Linda."

"Oh goody, is she back?"

"Well, no actually, she isn't yet," my dad murmured.

"Then does she have to stay longer or something, because that's fine."

"No not that either, she has well, um, passed away," Dad quietly said. A rush of disbelief filled my body. I had hope before, but now that was gone.

I WAS RELEASED from hospital a few days later. Excitement washed over me as I saw the familiar faces of my family and friends, their warm embraces wrapping me up in a blanket of happiness. As I stepped into the car, I glanced back at the hospital, remembering Linda, the true hero that helped me conquer those few weeks. She was the person that saved me, that kept me company. And because of that, I will never forget her.

26

THE LIFE OF A GUINEA PIG

BY NOVA MACKNIK-CONDE

T his fiction story is inspired on real events from the lives of my two guinea pigs, Oreo and Snickerdoodle, who were rescued from Prospect Park in Brooklyn, New York, late last year.

Oreo sniffled. His human family had taken him and his brother, Snickerdoodle, here to die. Oreo didn't really know where 'here' was, but it was probably something like the wilderness. It was late fall, and soon he and Snickerdoodle would freeze to death, in a cold, lonely place, with no food, no water, no shelter, no nothing. The last thing Oreo saw before his family took him away was a small brown puppy, yapping at them. Oreo could only speculate, but he suspected that the puppy was to be their replacement. It was a terrible day to be a small, fragile, soon to be preyed upon, guinea pig.

Because Snickerdoodle was brown, he could camouflage a bit better with the forest around them, but noooo, he just had to have their only hiding place, which wasn't even really a hiding place, just a tiny twig that didn't even cover a square inch of either of their bodies. Oreo was black and white, the exact opposite of their surroundings, so if a hawk or another predator came, he would be eaten immediately. Oreo started to cry. But then, a mysterious guinea pig appeared out of nowhere. It looked almost exactly like Oreo.

"Don't be scared!" The new guinea pig oinked.

"*Ahhhhh!*" Oreo screamed.

"Oh, come on, I *just told you*—you know what, never mind. Don't be sad that your humans abandoned you here because I'm you from the future! Everything will be okay! You'll get rescued by a kind human, who will take you to your forever family!" Future-Oreo oinked happily, jumping for joy.

"But what about Snickerdoodle?" Oreo asked.

"Yeah, what about me?" Snickerdoodle whimpered.

"Oh, don't worry! They'll take Snickerdoodle too!" Future-Oreo said. "Bye! Don't forget what I said!" He oinked as he faded away.

Right ten, a human walked up to them, gasping when she saw the two guinea pigs huddling together in fear. Oreo almost bolted but he remembered Future-Oreo's words, and he stayed put. The human walked away, but she returned just a few minutes later, and made a trail of treats on the ground leading to a bag. Oreo and Snickerdoodle were very hungry, so they ate the treats, and the human zipped the bag behind them. Oreo started to panic. He *hated* small spaces with all his might, but under his fear, he felt a sense of relief. Future-Oreo had not been lying. He and Snickerdoodle were being rescued.

***

Many months later, Oreo snuffled around in the hay. He was now in a warm guinea pig habitat with lots and lots of yummy food, two water bottles, and even fresh fruit treats! It was a good day to be a guinea pig. He heard Snickerdoodle behind him, but he didn't look. Oreo felt something poke his butt, and he swivelled around. *Again?* Oreo thought. Snickerdoodle was the one that had poked him to get his attention, and now he was rumbling and slowly shaking his big, furry butt around the habitat. Oreo climbed on top of Snickerdoodle's head in a show of dominance, the guinea pig version of a chokehold, but he let his brother go after a few seconds. It was all in fun, and Snickerdoodle jumped for joy that he was free.

"Why are you popcorning, you silly?" Oreo oinked at him.

"Just because," Snickerdoodle oinked back.

Just then, a human opened the door to the room. It was their adoptive mommy, the one that took care of them and refilled their water bottles every morning. Oreo and Snickerdoodle stood up on the side of their cage and begged for treats. Oreo started to teeth chatter at the human out of excitement, but he stopped as soon as the human began to sprinkle apple bits around the cage. The human left, closing the door behind them, and Oreo and Snickerdoodle foraged for the treats. Just then a new piggy appeared out of thin air. It was... Oreo, but... older?

"You've got to be kidding me," Oreo oinked. It was Future-Oreo.

"Hey, guys! So I just want to tell you about when-" Future-Oreo began.

"No! Not again!" said Snickerdoodle and Oreo, but they both sat down to listen.

2021 8-11 CATEGORY WINNER

GUEST STORY - UNTHEMED

27

RED BEAN BUNS

BY ESTHER LI

"Julie, you have to attend," my mum said.

I SPRAWLED across my bed and buried my damp face in the silk sheets. My throat felt thick
   and heavy, as if laden with words I did not know how to express. Only a small sob escaped.

"WO BU YAO!" I shouted. *I don't want to.*

"YOU HAVE TO. You're his friend. He would have wanted you to say goodbye."

. . .

I PRESSED my lips together and stood up, slamming my bedroom door behind me as I followed my mother to the car. She wore a long black dress and a single white flower in her hair. She pinned a small chrysanthemum to mine. Its pale white petals felt as fragile as my heart. My dad was already in the car, a stony expression on his face as he gripped the steering wheel tightly.

WE SPENT the car ride in heavy silence and I sat there simmering in my frustration as I thought about having to attend a ceremony that solidified Hu's death as a concrete reality. Languishing at home and distracting myself with baking, I could almost imagine him still there at his own house, baking his favourite Chinese sweets, always just a phone call away.

WHEN WE ARRIVED at the funeral, we sat down at our designated seats. Before us, rows and rows of white flower wreaths were placed next to a large black casket at the centre of the room. Above it was a black and white photograph of Hu's smiling face.

HU WAS ALWAYS SMILING. He always shone so brightly, even near the end when he was kept alive by tubes down his nose.

"ONE DAY we're going to build the bakery of our dreams! Together!!" Hu would exclaim with his thin arms in the air and brown eyes sparkling. "You can do the Western style cupcakes and I can make the mochi and the egg tarts and the red bean buns!"

"I DON'T REALLY THINK we'll be successful," I would say with a wrinkle of my nose. "Keeping a store open seems hard. What if they don't like our food?"

. . .

"OF COURSE they'll love the food! Who wouldn't love red bean buns!"

I CHOKED up thinking about Hu's dreams as I stared at the black casket that now imprisoned them. I shouldn't have come today. It was too painful. I stood up and ran outside before his father could take the podium and start the ceremony. I ran past his mother, who I hadn't seen much ever since he passed away.

I USED to see Hu's family every day. We would go to his house after school to do our homework and then on some days, he'd bake his favourite red bean buns. I always helped him crush the bean paste and knead the dough.

"STAY FOR DINNER," his mum would say. "We always love having you over."

SHE WOULD WAVE me over to try her stir fry and throughout dinner Hu's dad would often compare the two of us, as all Asian parents did.

"HU, why can't you be more like Julie?" he would say. "She always gets top marks in class."

I MISSED HU'S FAMILY. They were like a second family to me.

. . .

I KNELT DOWN NEXT to the building and started to sob. Wet tears cascaded down my cheeks as I cried so hard, I felt as if I was gasping for breath. I hoped no one I knew could hear me.

BY THE TIME I had calmed down and headed back inside, the ceremony had ended. It was better this way; I didn't want to see his face, his lifeless body. A procession of people lifted the casket and walked down the hallway, where it loaded onto a hearse. We followed it via car to the burial site.

I WATCHED as they lowered Hu's casket into the dark earth beyond. One by one we scattered white chrysanthemum petals onto the casket as his parents stood there, red eyed and streaked with tears.

"JULIE," his mum said when it was my turn. "It's good to see you again. You should visit us again sometime. We miss you."

"SORRY I HAVEN'T COME OVER," I said. "I miss you guys too."

I WATCHED the scattered petals descend into the swallowing darkness like drifting snow on a cold winter's night. After we had all said our goodbyes, dirt was shovelled on top of the grave. We headed to the altar, a small structure next to the grave with a pit for burning paper money, dirt for placing incense and a decorative plate for food offerings.

"HERE, JULIE," Hu's dad said as he opened a small plastic box. "Take some red bean buns to share with Hu."

· · ·

I TOOK TWO BUNS, one which I placed on Hu's altar and took a small bite out of the other. The taste on my lips was soft and sweet as I finally gulped it down. Hu's dad lit a small fire inside the altar pit. It flickered in the afternoon sun as Hu's mum handed everyone a stack of paper money to burn.

I KNEELED and fed note by note by note into the fire. The hot breath of burning embers touched my cheek as a small wisp of smoke floated up towards the blue sky. I hoped the money would reach Hu in the afterlife.

I EXHALED DEEPLY. Maybe attending the funeral wasn't so bad after all. I felt a strange sense of calm and a deeper connection to the people that loved Hu just as much as I did.

"HU," I said. "I hope you're still as happy as always, somewhere out there. I promise I will open the bakery we always dreamed about."

I STARED at the red bean bun on Hu's altar and smiled for the first time since he left us.

AGES 12-16 WINNERS & COMMENDED ENTRIES

28

AN ODE TO THE VULTURE

BY BAKER T. BEAUREGARD

1st Place in 12-16 category

For Paco

Vehicular feline-slaughter in 10 steps:

1. Hear a soft thunk.
2. Pause (dread).
3. Curse.
4. Pull forward.
5. Hesitate.
6. Get out of the car.
7. Curse (dirtier this time).
8. Pause (respectful).
9. Pause (heinous).
10. Hide the body.

Our neighbor lived in a small yellow house, her lawn so over-grown, so sprinkled with tires and trash, that you had to be wary of snakes and glass as you approached her door. Where there are snakes, there must be mice. Where there are mice, there must be cats. And where there are crazy yellow-housed neighbors, there is a tendency to feed and name each of these cats. These are the laws of the universe.

The one I killed was named Paco. He was one of seventeen cats, but he would be missed. He was fond of graham crackers and ESPN, as this neighbor would later tell us, missing posters in hand, her words swallowed in grief, and her mascara leaving black streaks down her cheeks.

Shame, shame. We will keep an eye out for him. He'll turn up. He'll turn up.

Paco would not turn up.

I was the one to move him. He was flattened, his brown coat wet and stained with red, and an odd pink liquid running from where his stomach had burst. I had never liked gore, but I had no problems that day. There is a criminal in each of us, hiding just behind the eyes, ready to harden the stare and forget what needs to be forgotten.

My brother vomited. His inner criminal is shy.

I dragged Paco behind the oak tree in the backyard beside a patch of bluebonnets. We considered burying him, but by the time I had power washed the blood from the driveway and tire, I was no longer a criminal. I was a child again, a child who should not have been driving her father's car. A child who was rather fond of cats. I cried in the shower as I washed the Murder from my skin, tears mixing with the water and evaporated Malice.

Three vultures ate Paco. They arrived together, looking oddly like bald businessmen in fine black suits, and eagerly swarmed his fly-covered corpse for a half hour before they made their move. I watched them from the dinner table, my meatloaf becoming increasingly unappetizing.

It took them just a day to devour him down to the bone. Those carrion kings, their beaks full of murdered meat, their cool white eyes watching me knowingly as they ate without chewing. They took no pleasure in it. They ate with no hunger, but with mechanical efficiency—three businessmen with work to do. There is no better way to hide the truth than to swallow it and let it dissolve into silence. They would not tell. My brother would never tell. Yellow-Housed neighbors would never know.

Shame, shame. We will keep an eye out for him. He'll turn up. He'll turn up.

I drive through these streets sometimes, where the grass turns yellow and the only sounds are the fly-warring cattle's battle cries, and I see them. Oiled black wings on Bastrop wind. Circling, circling, circling. Silent. Promising, promising, promising. While I see nothing but sandpaper grass and cat-tongue bush beneath them, I know there is death here, quiet as it may be.

This is an ode to the vulture
To the songless dukes of death
To the devourers of the dirty
To the roadkill royals
They remember so we may forget

I dip my head to you when we pass one another on the highway.
Remember Paco? I say, rolling down the window.
You turn to me and remain silent as you fly.
Of course you do. Of course. This is your job, and it's rude of me to ask.
How many secrets does it take to fill your belly? I cry.
And you say nothing because you don't know.

29

THE WHEELBARROW

BY SAADYA LEBENS

2nd Place in 12-16 category

First came the stench, the reek of something that was once alive, rotting. Then came the clatter, the bumping, the sound of something with wheels rumbling down the cobbled roads. Then came the light of a hooded lantern, a dim halo that spoke of cheap oil. Then came a large wheelbarrow, heaped with corpses, and a man in an avian mask pushing it. The bodies that had been haphazardly thrown into the wheelbarrow were covered in blackened bulbous swellings, most leaking a rancid-smelling pus. Some of the bodies were fresh, others falling apart.

The man pushing the wheelbarrow wore a black cloak. The beak of his mask was filled with strong-smelling herbs, but even they could not fight off the stench of the black death. His name was Hugh. The year was 1351. The end of the world, as far as Hugh was concerned. That was what any priest worth his breeches was saying. People were dropping dead wherever you looked.

The streets of London were filthy, covered in excrement, spit, and other unsavoury things. The air was smoky and oppressive, and the lights were out. A body slumped in a back alley. Hugh walked over to the corpse, retched, and hauled him onto the wheelbarrow. And as the sun began to peek from underneath the world, waiting for the moon to retire, Hugh pushed his wheelbarrow. It held around a dozen corpses by now. He pushed it to a church, pushed it to the graveyard and pushed the rancid bodies into a massive pit.

The pit was deep, though you wouldn't be able to tell, as the corpses layered up to the top. Hundreds of them. Glazed over eyes, blood-soaked clothing, pus leaking from the swellings. There were countless hundreds of these pits, all around London.

Hugh walked back to his home, and as he did, the people he passed drew away from him. Mothers held their children close. Everywhere Hugh looked, distrustful eyes stared back. Tired and horrified eyes.

He knew what they said about his kind. They came at night, taking your loved ones.

But Hugh could imagine what it would be like *without* his sort. Streets piled high with rotting corpses, more and more people getting sick, adding to the piles of death. It wasn't as if Hugh enjoyed his work. But people would be people. Always needing a scapegoat.

As Hugh reached his house a group of young men at his door looked up. They held knives.

"I don't want any trouble," Hugh said as he took a step back.

One of the men grabbed him and slammed his face into the door. There was a snap as Hugh's mask splintered, and as Hugh stumbled, two men grabbed him from behind, as a third brought back his blade to thrust.

Hugh shoved himself free and ran to his door as the third man stabbed at empty air. Hugh opened his door, darted inside, and bolted it. He heard the thud of the men's footsteps outside. Then silence.

He sat down and removed his shattered mask, revealing a gaunt and malnourished face with sunken brown eyes. Herbs and flowers fell from the black wood as he laid it down on his table.

He looked down at his hands. The tips of his fingers had blackened. This was what he had feared since the black death began. All men fear death, and for a moment Hugh felt a wave of dread. But no, there was work to be done. He had known the dangers of his occupation. He had dug his own grave. Somewhere deep down he knew this was coming. And it was a price he paid willingly. There was work to be done.

First came the stench, the reek of something that was once alive, rotting. Then came the clatter, the bumping, the sound of something with wheels rumbling down the cobbled roads. Then came the light of a hooded lantern, a dim halo that spoke of cheap oil. Then came a large wheelbarrow, heaped with corpses, and a woman in an avian mask pushing it.

Alice walked the darkened streets and she saw the end of the world. The end she was trying to fight. No matter what her family thought of it. Far off, she saw a corpse hunched over an empty wheelbarrow.

A man in a shattered mask.

30

THE SACRIFICE OF KUYILI

BY DHARSHWANA MURALIDHARAN

3rd Place in 12-16 category

The heat of the noon sun burns the soles of my feet, but it makes me faster. I tightly grip the wicker basket over my head, teeming with goods. My heart burns with determination but also fear. I turn to look at the rest of Udayal Padai. They're adorned with colourful bead jewellery and sweet-smelling jasmine flowers on the tops of their braids, just like all the other women walking down this road. Except we all have a desire to take back what's ours.

We march on, towards the Sivagangai Palace with its red turrets and white exterior. It's teeming with British guards. Grim expressions are etched onto their foreign faces. Their green uniforms and lathis look outlandish in all the brightly coloured saris and kurtas of those celebrating Vijayadashami. The line for entering the palace's temple reaches till the eye's end, and street vendors dot the line, selling goods.

I slip in through the sweaty bodies and reach a brown tented stall,

I ask for a jar of ghee. The vendor gives me a toothy smile and says: "What evil influences are you hoping to get rid of, eh?"

I give him a small smile and turn to once again sift through the mass of bodies to reach the rest of the women. Little does he know that the bottle of ghee will get rid of more

than he expects. I lower the basket from the tip of my head and tuck the bottle of ghee next to the flower garland.

Just as I am securing it onto my head again, Queen Velu Nachi-yar's carriage rumbles down the road. I signal the rest of Udayal Padai to follow me. The queen gets off the carriage, and we get behind her.

She turns towards me. "Kuyili, the sacrifice you will make tonight will never be forgotten." A kind smile fills her face, and she announces to the rest of Udayal Pdai with her clear and beautiful voice: "Fight hard, for the sake of your freedom and for our brave soul Veera Managai Kuyili." With that, she turns back towards the palace.

I see that the guards are tightening their grip on their latis. I force myself to plaster on an innocent smile. A guard with a cropped brown moustache waves his hand towards my basket. I swallow my fear.

I repeat the English words Queen Velu taught us. "Offering God," I say. The words feel sour and misplaced in my mouth, but they seem to satisfy the guard as he lets us enter.

We reach the statue of Ramma, the Udayal Padai and I lay out the contents of all our offerings. All that's left in the basket is a red blanket and the jar of ghee, or so it may seem.

The queen tells the British guard that she will leave, but the rest of Udayal Pdai will stay to pray more. He gives a curt nod and follows her out.

As soon as the queen's emerald green sari is out of sight, we reach for our wicker baskets once again. But this time, we don't take out flowers or bananas, but our blades. I shout to the rest of the Udayal Padai, "Let us get back what was ours!" They all nod and run out, blades in hand. The perfect distraction.

I take out the ghee and a matchbox from the bottom of my basket. It's time. I run through the stone temple, weaving past the pillars, and hurrying down a dimly lit staircase. I push open the wooden doors, revealing the armoury.

Rows of blades and pistols fill the room on wooden shelves. The British guards will come soon to gather their weapons to take the lives of Udayal Padai. I am too weak to defeat them on my own, but I can get rid of it all. It will only come to me one thing. My life.

I open the jar of ghee and slather it all over my body. I open the crook of my left palm to see the matchbox. With one swift move, a fire comes alive. The fire that will take my life, but the fire that will give others one freedom. I drop it to the ground.

Slowly it will spread, getting rid of the weapons.

Queen Velu's words come back to me, "The sacrifice you will make tonight will never be forgotten."

Will they remember? The sacrifice and the fight that started it all.

GLOSSARY:

Udayal Padai: An army consisting of only women assembled by Queen Velu.

Ghee: A condiment similar to butter, normally sold in temples as offerings to God that will get rid of evil influences.

Vijayadashami: A holiday in India commonly celebrated by women, to symbolize Ramma the Indian God's triumph against Ravanna who is a devil.

31

A NORMANDY BEACH

BY ELLIE KARLIN

Highly Commended in 12-16 category

The candle gleamed with an angry light. The flame grew with every passing moment. I knew it wanted nothing more than to sink its teeth into my flesh.

Dead man, the candle hissed at me. *Just another dead man.*

I felt its heat on my face, and then I was burning, my skin alive with heat, even as my frail body shook and my teeth rattled. I shivered all over. There was pain, smoking, freezing pain that covered me like red paint. Once, I thought I understood pain, but that was before, when I was young. Strong. Powerful.

I was breathing quickly. Too quickly. I couldn't stop. The breaths were agony but they kept coming. Each lungful squeezed through my oesophagus.

Dead man, the candle whispered, *just another dead man.*

The flame was so close and so big. It loomed over me. My chest rose and fell in juddering gasps. I screamed and figures rushed in. I tried to tell them about the candle, but it came out as another scream.

I screamed myself into oblivion.

When I woke up, the world was very bright.

I was standing on a beach, the sun blazing down, and for one glorious moment I thought I was free. Then I sniffed the air. Mixed in with the ocean's salty tang was the long-forgotten stench of death.

Staring around in horror, memories rose from the ashes. For the second time in my life, I looked upon a yellow beach strewn with corpses. They littered the sand like chewing gum wrappers, dead and empty. Some of their mouths gaped open. They had died screaming. Some of the faces were shrivelled and decayed. Some of them didn't have faces at all. I stared into their eyes, those who had them. Brown, blue, green, grey, black, it didn't matter. They all stared up at the sky, unseeing, and I stared down at them.

Around me, living men were gathering bodies, dragging them up the beach. They moved like robots, stiff-limbed and automatic, but revulsion and pity lined their faces.

Then I was among them, cradling the dead in my arms, loading them onto carts. Men around me were speaking softly to each other. I tried to speak too, but the scene was already dissolving.

We were building some structure, nearly finished. My arms ached from the strain, but my fingers worked on. A makeshift cemetery, I remembered as I stepped back.

I could hear the sea behind us. And then there were the bodies, brought here to rest. People were praying around me.

Bile rose in my throat and I felt a familiar despair. Was this all life was? Some twisted joke where some men sought glory cutting each other down and other men stooped to pick up the pieces?

I looked at the living. Their faces were gaunt and frightened. A job nobody wanted, a job as necessary as it was sordid. I felt infected as I laid down corpse after corpse, as if their deadness was seeping into my life, sucking it away.

"Someone has to do it, Joey, why not us? The dead must be honoured, even in war."

The man's voice filled my head, a friend once, yet now far away. I felt I would soon see him again.

I heard different voices now, soft, calling from a different world.

My world. This cemetery was no longer my world. It ran on like a film, and I watched it.

Over, I thought. *Yes, over. You did your duty. You were no hero, just a gravedigger. But now your own grave awaits you.*

Faces from my past, dead and living, floated in front of me for one long moment, then I shuddered and awoke. The pain blazed once again, but the dark room was crowded with faces I loved.

"Memories," I murmured hoarsely.

My son and his family looked at me. I couldn't see any of them too clearly anymore but I felt the youngest girl's curious stare.

Weary but smiling, I knew myself to be an old, old man. "We buried them all, and so few still alive remember. None sing to remember the men who spent their days with corpses while others fought. But the dead must be honoured, even in war... yes, even in war."

32

EQUIPPING FOR A BRIGHTER FUTURE

BY CHLOE HUERIN SUH

Highly Commended in 12-16 category

The sandwich was exceptionally delicious that morning. Toasted onion bagel nice and crusty covered in mayo on one side and pesto on the other, added with crispy bacon, avocado with a pinch of lemon pepper, and a sunny side egg, it was a taste of heaven as the yoke drips down my fingers. I check the time on my phone as I munch on my sandwich. My dimension of bliss came to a screeching halt with a shocking revelation that it was already 7:17. I had three minutes to catch the school bus.

I jumped up, wiped off the yoke and the breadcrumbs, grabbed my bag, and bolted out of the house catching the elevator. The elevator began from the B1 floor and counted one, two, three... It was going to take a while to reach thirty-two. I was not going to make it. In a panic, I texted my friend who had taken the bus from the previous station, pleading if he could ask the bus driver to wait just two minutes.

"He says hurry!"

Ding. As soon as the elevator door opened, I raced down the apartment complex. I gasped for air and began to feel lactic acids building up in my legs. I turned the corner and identified the small yellow bus with the emergency signal waiting for me. I mustered all my strength and sprinted the last 100 meters like the ones I had seen in the Olympics. My backpack jiggling uncontrollably from behind and my hair looking wild as it can be, it must have been a sight to see for those waiting on the bus.

"Good morning! Having a rough start?"
"Yeah... Thank you for waiting," I sheepishly exclaimed, still gasping for air.

His big smile and kind gesture caught me off guard as I entered nervously, expecting some sort of a scolding. His warmness was actually quite comforting. As I sat in the back seat, still catching my breath, I knew my day would be just fine. The bus arrived at school, and I thanked him again for waiting for me. He wished me a great day and told me to learn as much as possible. Perhaps, a bit cliche, yet his words carried so much genuineness that they touched my heart. Then, I realized that all this time, the bus drivers picked us up to school, candidly wishing that all of us would learn and grow as much as possible.

A moment of flashbacks reminded me that he always smiled; I just didn't take the time to notice. Some days I would be discouraged by under-delivered test results, and he would ask me if I was having a bad day. Down casted, I would reply, "I didn't do so well on my test." "It's okay; you can do well next time," he would exclaim. I didn't know it then, but I realized that behind those small talks and initiatives was a deeply caring heart cheering and rooting for all of us.

There are thousands of bus drivers and taxi drivers where I live. They serve as a backbone to the community, transporting countless people day in and day out. I've always appreciated them but never expressed my appreciation or acknowledged them beyond job descriptions. One thing was certain. Beyond transporting us back and forth, our bus driver was equipping us for a brighter future.

3:15 pm finally arrived. Just like any other day, our bus driver was right there waiting for us, pleasantly smiling. However, this time I noticed. "Had a great day?" He asked. "I had a wonderful day! Thank you so much!" I said it with the biggest smile and meant every word.

AGES 12-16 LONG LISTED STORIES

33

YOUNG HEROES

BY SHOUMIK MANTHANA

Most people consider the rural town of Mylavaram located in southern India, to be one of rugged nature, stressing agriculture to fuel the city's vitality. Surrounded by looming mountainous barriers and seemingly endless farmland, the city's civilians live in districts of villages where a small home could double as schooling for over 100 hundred kids. This summer, I visited Mylavaram in what was considered the peak of its torrid weather. Along with my family, we spent the duration of our stay at a local housing business in order to commute to the temple that was getting inaugurated nearby. In all honesty, the blistering heat was some of the hottest and most difficult conditions I have ever been in, let alone living and partaking in daily activities! With the help of the ever-trustworthy air conditioning system, and other handheld cooling systems, we would commute to the temple every day and undergo the ritual that was a part of the inauguration process.

Part of the event was a project conducted by the children from the U.S.A to deliver about a thousand backpacks filled with materials and school supplies to the students of the district village. A band of about

5 kids including myself would sit in a dining room every day and pack about 200 backpacks till completion. The exhausting process took about 2 days to complete. The backpacks were loaded into a tractor for transportation throughout the district's schools. I was lucky enough to sit in the passenger seat near the front of the vehicle, whereas the rest of my peers watched the contents of the backpacks in the back of the vehicle all while over 105°F of heat surely took effect. We arrived at the first school and unloaded the boxes into one of the classrooms of what looked like a kindergarten. The building itself was tiny, but what really amazed me was that such a small structure was housing over 50 students seated on muddy flooring, with little to no ventilation, and only one instructor acting as a teacher for all of the kids. At the sight of visitors, the students and teachers alike were curious as they walked out into a small pavilion. Most children did not wear footwear, and the individuals that did wear battered sandals provided little immunity to the blistering grounds. Their uniforms were neat and identical, their faces filled with an inquisitive nature and excitement at a new surprise and chance to learn something new. With one stern but loving order from a teacher, they all sat down in spick rows of 4 and said their greetings in unison. We stated our purpose, and the teachers translated the message to the students. And at that moment, I would witness something that I will most definitely remember for the rest of my life. The students cheered in excitement, their faces lit up and they rejoiced as they showed their gratitude for all but a unisex backpack with a few candies and materials. They all said their thanks and eagerly waited for the pack. In the US, I had been given everything I needed and wanted by my parents and the people around me. The resources, environment, friends, and way of life were something that I began to think I took advantage of.

The kids of the U.S.A project visited an intermediate and high school shortly after kindergarten. In comparison, a high schooler in the 12th grade would be about the same size as an elementary or middle schooler in the U.S due to the lack of nutrition and other resources readily available in the states. During my short encounters

34

LANGADU

BY DIVYAM DAVE

Brown fuzz crossed the corner of my eye and I caught two deer running in my backyard. Of course, this was a common occurrence; however, this time, one of the deer had its back legs twisted the wrong way. I noticed that its two back legs were bent backwards, resulting in the deer moving only with its front two feet. Baffled, I sprinted to grab a camera after rummaging through a box of tangled tech supplies only to come back and find that the deer had vanished from the scene.

I once again saw two deer the next day. Immediately, I scanned their legs and found that the deer with the twisted back legs had returned. I pointed this out to my family, and all their heads turned in awe to look at the deer.

"Poor little Langadu," my mother muttered as we slowly got back to our meal.

Langadu, in my family's native language, Gujurati, means "a person or thing that limps". That nickname caught on and we would continue to refer to the deer that way.

After a few months, the deer looked unwell. My mom suggested that Langadu might be pregnant. The deer was visibly struggling to move around, but still managed to eat and traverse into the forest to rest. Not more than two days later, Langadu returned with two young fawns. My mom had been right. Unfortunately, the deer looked very unwell after giving birth. As its two children ran and frolicked in the yard, she barely stood on her two front legs and merely watched from a distance.

With time, the deer's condition worsened. We told our neighbour's and contacted some animal experts about the deer. They said that it was best for the deer to remain in its natural habitat and be undisturbed as it was still living somewhat normally.

The deer's mother continued caring for her children, who did not seem to have any disabilities. By this time, I was a bit older and had more understanding of the world. This led me to do some research on the internet. I found an image that went along with an article explaining this problem with the deer's legs. It stated that they were most likely broken and had never healed.

On the way to a tennis tournament, I told my family about what I had read. As if it was the deer's calling, about a minute later, we saw Langadu grazing in a grassy field on the left side
of the road. There was a group of deer with Langadu, and they seemed to be helping her around and protecting her because of her disability.

"Wow, I can't believe we are seeing this! It's straight off a National Geographic documentary!" my sister exclaimed.

After we got back from the tournament, I couldn't get the journey of Langadu the deer out of my head. As a human I could not imagine having to take care of two children while barely being able to walk. It made me think long that night about how courageous that deer was. It struggled, but still managed to raise its young and seek assistance from the other deer. Langadu taught me a lesson that I couldn't have learned any other way. No matter the struggle or hardship, animals in nature have their choices limited to rest or to seek out alternative methods. They must do what runs in their blood, a resiliency for survival.

We started to see the deer less and less over time, and finally, we never saw Langadu again. Although the story likely will not be

35

THE BOY

BY AMY GRACE

I had a hero once. His name was Tyler James. But unlike most heroes his name wasn't written in any of the history books, he didn't have millions of adoring fans desperate for even a glimpse of him. In fact I think I'm the only person who ever knew the real Tyler James, aside from the drug and the alcohol, his addiction.

Tyler grew up in a loving home for the start of his life, his parents adored him as did everyone who met him. It wasn't hard to love him. He had a way of seeing life in all its beauty, he loved the things most people hated. He loved the rain because it showed him that, like us, the world is far from perfect. His Dad and him always used to play guitar at sunset, they loved the story a song could tell, the wonderful simplicity of a song that could drive someone to tears by a few mere words. They played every night, singing to the glistening stars splattered across the murky night sky. At least they did before his Mom left, and his father became consumed by alchohol. But Tyler was fine, he had new company, in the form of a white powder called heroin. It made him feel safe and loved, kept him warm like an old blanket, sheltering him for his problems. He told himself he wasn't addicted, but then once a day became seven times a day. The drug was no longer a want, it was a need, he needed to feel like nothing in the world could stop him. He needed that unstoppable rush of euphoria. He needed a break from the cruel moments' life had in store for him.

That was when I met him. I saw him sitting across from me at a party, his deep cobalt blue eyes were sunken and bloodshot. His cheeks gaunt from the lack of eating. And that's when he met my gaze. I don't know how long we were like that for, frozen, lost in each other's gaze, until he finally approached me. We talked for hours, like we had known each other for years. The Buddhists say when you finally meet your soulmate you're hit with a state of tranquility, you finally feel calm, almost as if there weren't a worry in the world. That's how I felt when I met Taylor James. We went out almost every night - carnivals, picnics, bars, long walks - it didn't matter as long as we were together. I loved him for who he was and in turn he did the same for me. I struggled with eating back then. I'd convince myself that I didn't need to eat, that I was fine. I wasn't fine. I was shutting everyone out and letting this monster, in disguise of a friend, consume me and control everything I did. My family weren't supportive, I could feel their judgment with every cold-hearted stare at my fragile body. Acting as though they didn't have time for me or my problems.

'You call that beautiful, Harper?'

But Tyler was different. He loved me, and he was, in the end, the only person who could save me from myself. He told me I would get through this, that I would get past the monster consuming me whole. And I did, despite everything, I did.

'You're more than your body, Harp. You're so beautiful, don't ever let anyone tell you otherwise.'

But I didn't realize that he hadn't beaten his own monster.

TYLER JAMES DIED in August 1973 from a drug overdose. His heart simply couldn't take it. And I regret it, I regret not trying to help him like he helped me. I would've done anything for that boy, I would've ripped my heart in two, but that simply wasn't enough. It breaks my heart to know that the world will never know the wonderful boy called Tyler James, whose voice could light up an entire room, whose eyes shone at every sunset, a boy who was kind and caring, whose words saved my life and brightened my world in every way possible. And I will always love him.

FOREVER AND ALWAYS.

36

M&M'S

BY NATALIE GHARIBIAN

J uly 29th, 2015. My mom entered the kitchen from the garage door, teary eyed, after picking up my brother from cross-country practice. I was merely seven years old, an innocent and pure kid who was concerned for my mother. She then broke the heart-breaking news that my great-grandmother Rosa had passed away. Attributable to my young age, I hadn't really understood entirely what had happened. I had never endured a loss before and, frankly, it was all so new to me. I recall asking my mother what had happened, and where my great-grandmother went. She told me that Rosa Tatik, a nickname we called her in Armenian meaning Grand-mother Rosa, was gone. I was perplexed and didn't quite comprehend what she meant by her being gone. My mom, Armine, then continued to illustrate that even though physically she was gone from this world, she would always remain in our hearts and make sure we're safe by watching over us. From that moment onward, I finally realized what occurred. She was never going to come back to me, nor to my family. Eventually, I was told stories about her life by my grand-mother and mom. I became informed of Rosa's incredible life full of a myriad of journeys, which I will never forget.

Red. Strong leader. Determined. Assertive. Risk-taker. Rosa was an exceptionally hard worker and always persistent. Rosa was a talented seamstress, and worked hours sewing and designing clothing for hundreds, if not thousands, of women to wear. Overall, she took risks and was the chief provider for her family.

Orange. Encouraging. Optimistic. Comforting. Excitement. Rosa Tatik held strong enthusiasm and passion for her grandkids and great grandkids. She made sure we were nurtured and cheerful. Despite her own hardships, she was inevitably sanguine and supportive.

Green. Inventive. Logical. Perfectionist. Rosa exhibited her creativity and innovation through her cooking, which she absolutely loved doing for her family, and through creating dresses from scratch. Although Rosa did not like to read, she was intelligent by way of her imagination. She sowed any cloth she could get her hands on. Her son would send her magazines, such as Vogue, from the States. She would fabricate dresses based off of these magazines and would sell them to her clients. From her work, she kept the household together and strong.

Blue. Caring. Enthusiastic. Sincere. Rosa cherished her family and was always seen with them. She would always take care of her loved ones every day. She was truly generous and altruistic.

Yellow. Illuminating. Friendly. Rosa Tatik had a great number of friends who deeply admired her. In addition, she loved having guests over, whether they were her friends or family.

Dark brown. Resilience. Security. Dependability. Great-Grand-mother Rosa remained headstrong for the people around her and never displayed weakness or fragility. While with her kids, grandkids, etc., Rosa always conveyed a sense of safety and certainty.

My great-grandmother was born in Lebanon. She married my great-grandfather at a young age. They then moved to Armenia, specifically the municipal community in the north-eastern area of Armenia called Alaverdi. They lived on a farm with absolutely noth-ing. Therefore, it was crucial for my great-grandparents to work, so they could make enough to at least live a well-rounded life in the town. It was very difficult for my great-grandmother, who was practi-cally still a child. She began to sew on the farm and learned to cook delicious foods. She is my unsung hero. Albeit not being in history books or stories told around the world, my great-grandmother is a heroine for what she went through. Her actions went vastly unnoticed by me when I was younger, now, however, I get it. I understand all the tough times she went through, and I praise her for keeping a smile on her face no matter the circumstance.

Red. Orange. Green. Blue. Yellow. Dark Brown. All the traditional colors of M&M's. One of my most treasured memories of Rosa Tatik was that whenever I saw her, no matter the time or day, she would invariably give me M&M's. She would never give any other candy. Every single time I eat the candy now, I think back to her, all the memories I've made, and my younger self. The young me who didn't understand why she left and where she went. To this day, I miss her, but I remind myself, "Those we love never truly leave us."- Jack Thorne.

37

VEDEM; A STORY OF PERSEVERANCE

BY ZACH KING

I n 1943, the King of Denmark, Christian X, demanded and was permitted an inspection of the concentration camp known as Terezin, 30 miles north of Prague in the Czech Republic. Although rumours of the horrific conditions in camps like these were widespread, when the King's inspectors entered Terezin, they only saw what appeared to be a prosperous community filled with people living in relative peace and comfort. What the inspectors saw was also all a complete lie.

From 1942 to 1944, a group of teenage boys imprisoned in Terezin created a secret society called The Republic of Shkid to publish the longest-running underground magazine in a Nazi camp. The magazine was called Vedem, which means "In the Lead" in Czech. While being forced to withstand the brute of the Nazis, the boys continued to write, draw, edit and publish the magazine to secretly share amongst themselves every Friday night in their prison cell. By risking their lives to publish a first-hand account inside the camp, the boys were truly unsung heroes.

The contents of Vedem's earliest issues ranged anywhere from reviews to cartoons and humour pieces, aimed to lift up the boys' fellow spirits and pass the time. However, as the years went on,

Vedem began to report on more serious matters facing the ghetto's inhabitants. These reports include articles about feelings of homesickness, a loss of their own childhoods, and numerous self-reflections on the group's own mortality and abhorrent experiences, like transporting dead bodies to Terezin's crematorium.

Vedem's writers also reported on the Nazi's attempts to utilize Terezin to hide their true actions from world leaders like the King of Denmark, while remarking on their anger and attempts to defy their captors as much as possible. While writing about such subjects and publishing such a magazine was punishable by death, the group also made the most of their surroundings by, for instance, making friends with some of the imprisoned artists making propaganda materials for the Nazis in order to smuggle art supplies for the magazine.

Vedem's founder and editor-in-chief, Peter Ginz, an artistic prodigy and author, lead the production and organization of the magazine. Ginz initially used an old typewriter to publish the first editions, however after it broke, Ginz resorted to writing and illustrating over 50 issues of Vedem purely by hand with supplies sent to him by his non-Jewish mother still living in Prague. Ginz also constantly urged his fellow contributors to write about everything they experienced at Terezin, allowing for the creation of harrowing articles, unfiltered poetry, and targeted columns straight from the minds of the boys.

In the one year anniversary issue of Vedem, Petr wrote, "we can be satisfied with Vedem that it educated a while legion of writers who grasped something we call the courage to write. Because to express yourself is the ultimate goal."

As the creation of Vedem was an extremely dangerous task, the group constantly had to use codenames like "Dynamo," "Baked Glasses," or "Cold-Blooded Horse" to conceal their identities. The creation of the magazine itself was done in extreme secrecy from the guards, produced at a centre wooden table in their cell block or on their bunks while their friend's kept lookout. The hiding of editions in between the boys' bunks and the use of secret signals to signify if a

Nazi soldier was approaching were also necessary to protect the magazine and its creators.

Among the many who fought against Nazi Germany during the Second World War, these boys should be remembered as true unsung heroes, who in the face of death, chaos, and widespread destruction, showed courage and determination to create something that defied their captors and aimed to spread truth and hope. Out of the 92 boys who worked on Vedem, only 15 would survive the Holocaust, yet their writings, drawings and efforts show that even in the worst of situations, the truth shall prevail.

38

MY GREATEST HERO

BY SANJANA KOTAMRAJU

D earest Mum,

I wonder, why did you leave?

I never thought I was good enough. I know I'm not and that can't be denied. It's only now I understand.

I REALISED, and my world shattered like a glass cracking on hard ground. I realised I never treated you the way I should've. . .As I gaze up at the ineluctable nature of a million stars staring at my puny self, I cannot stop the guilt crushing me. Over and over and over again.

Because that's how bad my mistake was.

I never realised when you spent all those nights at extra shifts. I never got the thought when you made millions of calls to the same person. I remember you used to work long hours and amble home, frazzled – only to receive yells from me. You never raised your voice, never told me off. You said it was because I was 'working hard'. It only hit me now that I wasn't working.

You were.

We hadn't enough to even get by for dinner, going hungry daily. You used to run in the rain and strive to get bread most nights. I scolded you for giving me the same stuff every day. Bread. But I wouldn't have even got that if *you* hadn't starved yourself to feed me. I got a meal daily from fowlers - my boxing club. You gave the only food you had to me. Each midnight you shuddered and wept by yourself – dejected and greatly ailing, and *I* scolded *you* for being *lazy*. I am the world's greatest fool for I didn't know.

I didn't know how much you'd done for me.

You did all this to make me the world's greatest champion. You said *you* killed dad. I only now know you didn't.

I did, right?

I was the one who wanted to play with dad on the middle of the road that time I was two. I paid no heed when he warned me of danger. Then when a flaming orange jeep crashed into his frail body and left crimson trails, I was the one to blame. I punished you for my mistake, but what would it have mattered even if it was yours? I never remembered dad anyway.

I accused you, all my life. Loathed you. I was blinded by lustrous gold medals and waving my country's flag across a bewitching arena. I dreamed to become the world's greatest champion. You stayed up all those nights, endured flashes of merciless hitting, called the competition organiser despite the insults, directed the most sweet kindness at me. All behind the scenes, so I could enter the National finals. You adored me with a melting passion. You wanted for me to win because you trusted that I deserved it. You should've wished for my downfall for what I did. I had lived with you my whole life until fowlers took me to nationals. I remember how I scowled at you, looking back at you lovingly waving at me, thinking you wanted the finals' money. How I twisted your sweetness to bitter hatred in my own mind.

I did the finals, but I didn't get that lustrous, gold medal I had chased like a panting, lupine creature. I wasted all your sacrifices. I got barely second. Yet when I realised about all you did for me I knew I wasn't worth a silver medal. Let alone gold.

But when I realised it was too late.

I made the same mistake again. Even if you forgave me, I could never forgive myself for what I did... I hazily remember sprinting to our deteriorating house. I ran with stiff legs, all those memories of your smiles and laughs, your hugs and kisses, your affection and sacrifices, the distant times you picked me up and fed me. I approached your grave, just wishing you would do those things once more. I wept for the first time, like you did every night.

I dropped my silver medal, knelt, and cried a river at your feet. I bore your scarring wounds like an heirloom. I saw everyone else, staring. They never knew you were a hero or about what you did. No one knew, including me. I wanted to tell them.

I got the worst punishment; my own life was dead. I need you back.

I promise, I will be a better person. I will reconcile, I need you back mum.

I promise I'll hug you back. So please, forgive me.

39

FOUND HOPE

BY DHAVINA PRISKILA TJAHJADI

I found three pictures of that girl yesterday. They were stuffed inside a box deep within my closet. I had been rummaging through my past antics while preparing to move out for college when I caught the sight of her face on wrinkled polaroid film. It was that girl. The girl I once was.

She had sunken eyes. Eyes that were filled with torment, sorrow, and trouble. It was quite easy to find her in the crowd of same-aged people. Easy to find that one girl who's bony glare stares past your eyes and straight to the hollow void.

I picked up the first photo to inspect it further when I accidentally uncovered two more. Two more prints of my past. A past I so badly want to avoid, yet inevitably shaped me to the person I am today.

The second photo had been overlapping the third, leaving tiny space for the third photo to barely make an appearance before my eyes. I gently took the second photo in my hands and revealed an image of only the girl's arm. I vaguely remember her body, but through pictures, everything seemed to click back to memory all at once. Her arm was thin. Really thin. In fact, too thin. I remember the cold feeling that pushed against her ever-luscious hair on her arms, the feeling of resounding wave shocks in her head, the falling strands of hair from the point of her head, and the fatigue that never seemed to get away from her back after doing too many crunches for too long. In the photo, her arm was hooked to an IV drip. Something I remember she frequently had to do after fainting one too many times during PE or a simple trip to the supermarket.

The next photo was a picture of her smiling. A smile I hadn't seen in a while. It was a big and happy smile. The one you'd find in an audience-filled room of some comedy show. In this third photo, the girl looked far healthier. Her cheeks were more plump, her arms filled, and her waist wide. She was healthy. She was the girl who was slowly healing to become the person I am today.

Lilli. Lilli with a double 'L' and a hearty enunciation was her name. As I said before, Lilli was the girl I used to be. There's a profound abyss between the old and new Lilli. A chasm quite deep, you might not even recognize the personality I once was when compared to the character I am today.

Old Lilli had repeating visits to the psychologist, where she and Dr. Koleen would make false promises again and again just to be broken the next time they met. As you can tell, old Lilli wasn't a good promise-keeper, but she *was* a good secret-keeper. She kept every method of fasting she invented to herself and only herself. She guarded every knowledge about how many calories were contained in a banana or a grain of rice, safe inside her shrinking brain. A brain whose wide range of functions she used only to construct an impossible image for her body, for years without fail.

Like the detailed sharp edges of a ruby gem, I remember perfectly in detail what old Lilli used to do in her room. The things Lilli would do were unfound. Because Lilli was an unfound girl. A girl who was lost but needed greatly to be found.

She'd take her dog's new excrement bags and barf into them each time she was forced to eat. After each barf session, Lilli would then wipe her mouth and throw the stained white tissue into the same bag and hide it under her bed. She called it her 'barf stash'.

Slowly but surely, Lilli's BMI began dropping significantly. From a normal 23, it dropped to a solid 16. Through time, food tubes weren't enough. They had to sing songs to her about how good food tasted, how important food was, and how *I needed* to eat food. This method worked for a little while but then *I* relapsed – 2 times to be exact.

Steadily, *I* – Lilli slowly became more weighted and more lively. She got discharged the day of her birthday, March 13th. After some time, Lilli started transforming into me, the new Lilli. The unsung hero of my life, the unnamed soldier of my story. So, I say, thank you Lilli, for making me the person I am today.

40

THE JOURNALS OF OLIVER ABDALI

BY ALEXANDER VERMIILION

I first found the journals when I was ten years old. At the time I thought they were just stories, but now that I am older, I know that they are the only detailed accounts of the life of Oliver Abdali, and while he was not known to many, in these journals bound in leather his life is laid out for all who wish to view it.

I don't know if he and I are related, and I'm too afraid to speak his name to any but the paper before me. For after reading the slightly slanted words he left behind I know the story of his life. I know he wrote with his left hand, that he had brown eyes so dark they were nearly black, I know he loved the taste and crunch of almonds, I know he longed for the feel of cool water against his skin, and I know he wanted a new life somewhere in Scandinavia, a place of which he had only ever heard stories.

Oliver was half Afghan, have British, he was raised by his father in Afganistan, his mother died in childbirth and all he knew of her where stories passed down to him. He had a big brother too, though they did not get along. Only once did Oliver ever put his brother's name into writing, "Abdul and I fought today" he wrote in the messy handwriting of a child. After that he described a bloody fist fight between him and his brother in a park near their home. He discussed with the pencil how his brother had lost a tooth in the fight, and how Oliver and been ashamed as he limped home to his father. He gave extra detail to the other children that had chanted while brother fought brother. While his English was never perfect, and his handwriting was atrocious, he was observant.

Little details always found their way into his journals, especially in the one he wrote as a child. There are three journals, each written in a small book and stowed away in a tiny wooden box.

But one I always find my way back to is his last journal. It's here where he described fighting in a war he did not wish to fight. He described the vivid and gut-wrenching screams of children, the way he saw women left sobbing on the street as their veils were ripped from their heads and faces. And it was in this journal where he described being forced to shoot innocent and unarmed soldiers.

One of his final entries details how he was walking down the street with a rifle in his hands that he did not wish to carry when he saw a little girl. The girl had matted hair and a face smeared with dust and something that might have been blood. Oliver had set his gun on the ground and reached out his calloused hands toward the girl, he had only planned to offer her food that he had stashed in his pocket. But she had screamed in terror and ran down an alleyway, she had been afraid of a man who solely wanted to help her. "She was scared by the pattern on my clothes and the gun on ground." He wrote.

And in his very final entry, dated March 14, 2015, Oliver states that he plans to run away from the army that dragged him from his home and forced him to fire at soldiers he did not believe where his enemies. I do not know if he survived, all I know is that five years later I found his journals, stashed in a box underneath a hotel room bed. And that now you know at least part of the story of a man who was good underneath a horrible mask that had been glued to his face.

41

A CHRONICLE OF TRANSFORMATION

BY ANDREA MALPICA-ALCALA

August 19, 2021

A I had just come home from my first day of school in an entirely new country. I missed my old school, family, and the people I used to hang out with every day. I thought nothing could be worse than moving 2,000 miles away from my former home. My soul was tearing to pieces, and I just wanted to get my foregone life back.

September 25, 2021

I got offered a volunteering position at a musical theatre class for people with special abilities, varying from Down Syndrome, Autism Spectrum Disorder, amongst others. Since I was in serious need of community service hours for school, I gladly accepted. Nonetheless, I never expected to meet my ultimate inspiration in the form of one of the people I helped.

September 29, 2021

He was sitting on a big blue chair in the corner of the room, sharing his smile with everyone who walked by. What makes him extremely special, though, is that despite the countless limitations his body has to endure every day, he has a free, ambitious mind that inspires everyone. His name is Charles.

At first, I didn't expect him to be able to move around that much. However, as soon as I helped him put his shoes on, he stood up and walked to the *barre*, and started imitating the teacher's ballet moves. This was the first lesson Charles taught me: no matter how many limitations you may have in your life, you've got to find a way to keep on.

DECEMBER 13, 2021

After months of intensive rehearsals, we finally made our appearance at the winter showcase. I will never forget the smile that was drawn in his face throughout the entire show.

"One day, I'm going to be a professional actor," he said, as we were bowing to the applauding crowd.

That day, Charles taught me a second lesson: never stop believing in yourself, despite how impossible or difficult to reach your dreams may seem.

January 19, 2022

I returned from winter break, excited for the new production we were going to put up: *Aladdin*. Charles was quite excited and kept fighting for his dream of being a professional actor someday. His ability to keep on going always inspired me, and I admire him for that to this day.

MAY 31, 2022

I tested positive for Covid.

I couldn't believe it. I felt like my whole world was falling down in pieces: the show was one week away. I neatly folded and packed my costume and prepared to take it back to the theatre. I hoped that, by some miracle, I would test negative soon so I could at least go watch the show.

JUNE 6, 2022

I finally tested negative. I was extremely happy since I would be able to watch the finished production.

Everything was going out as planned. I was on cloud nine as I saw each of the actors remember each line and choreography. Charles walked onstage, but, as he was preparing to say his lines, he fell down.

I immediately felt the muscles in my entire body stiffen. My heart started pounding fastly as I saw him on the ground. As panic filled the room, I started telling myself that everything would be fine; he would overcome whatever had happened to him. The following minutes were full of silence.

Moments later, Charles reappeared from one of the entries, and everyone started clapping and cheering for him. He bowed a few times and gifted the audience the most genuine smile I've ever seen. After that, he continued performing as if nothing had happened. The fear that had formed inside of me finally came out in the form of tears. I realized the third lesson that Charles taught me is: every inconvenience is just a bump on the road; don't let it get on your way towards your goals and dreams.

Although I know I have helped Charles in many ways, he saved me from losing myself. If I hadn't met him, I wouldn't have gotten the inspiration to adapt to my life in the United States. I would've seen every insignificant obstacle as a gigantic impediment to accomplishing my goals. Ever since I met Charles, I've seen the challenges I face as "bumps on the road" that I can easily overcome if I put a little bit of perspective and ambition into each of my actions.

42

STEEL PEOPLE

BY MARIIA KALASHNYK

I want to tell you a story that, unfortunately, this year has touched the hearts and souls of every Ukrainian. A story about unsung heroes... about the defenders of Azovstal... I am very sorry that very little was said about them and the real catastrophe that took place in Mariupol, Ukraine.

In late February, Russia launched a war against Ukraine. One of the targets of the invaders was the coastal city of Mariupol. Unfortunately, the city was practically under occupation. All citizens and defenders were encircled, and this circle became smaller and smaller every single day. Our defenders were only a couple of thousand, and they opposed more than 10 thousandth horde, many times greater than their number. Over time, the circle narrowed and the Ukrainians remained only on the territory of the Azovstal, where were the most terrible battles in Europe over the past century. Our people were without food, water, medicine, they had no communication, no more weapons to defend. They were in an absolute besiegement, but they fought, stood, and held to the last! Even under every minute bombing with multi-ton bombs and incessant shelling they kept. This whole nightmare lasted 3 months... Our defenders showed just unprecedented courage and strength.

For me, the story is especially touching and heartbreaking, as they saved me, in fact, they saved my life. They took the whole blow, took away all the enemy's force, which was supposed to capture my city and let us prepare for defence. If not them, I don't know what would be with me now and where would I be now. I just can't convey how grateful I am to them. My heart bleeds every day for every defender who is in captivity. I pray and believe that they come home alive! In general, with their persistence, they protected many more cities of Ukraine and their inhabitants from active hostilities and occupation. And I think it's not right that the story of these unsung heroes remained in the shadows for many people.

I can't help but say about the firefighters, about the real heroes who are now, with their actions, in fact, saving the world from a terrible famine. These people put out fires in wheat fields after shelling, so that at least something can survive, and people won't die of hunger. These people sacrifice themselves, it's incredibly difficult, they work under bombardments, many of them are blown up by enemy mines. But everyone is silent about this anyway, silent about the exploits of these people, which they perform every day.

All these guys, they are real Heroes with a capital letter! Ukrainians will never forget their courage, strength, and self-sacrifice!

43

THE LIFE OF A FORGOTTEN AYAH

BY VARSHINI

From the blistering heat and the sweltering sun of Nagpur to the chilly breeze and the rainy city of London I travelled over the unpredictable, raging ocean. The five-month voyage from India to England had stolen much of my energy and my soul was already beginning to feel the effects of the British occupation in my great country of prosperity. My two brothers had already had their lives snatched away by a flurry of British bullets. Their crime? Not knowing English. A fury has been churning in my stomach from day one - calling to me, whispering vile thoughts in my ear, spreading animosity through my veins like a wildfire. But what can I do but remain silent as I have always done.

IT WAS in the scorching period of June of 1935 when I decided to sign myself up to the duty of an ayah. I already had experience with children helping to raise my younger sister and my deceased brother but when I explained this to my parents their tears still fell regardless. I already knew how to trick children into eating and how to play with them until their droopy eyelids closed and their tiny limbs stopped flailing and it was only a week before I found myself on a boat on which I was coaxed below deck with many more soon to be ayahs. Their eyes were alight with fear and one poor woman was curled up to the side in a ball swinging back and forth calling desperately for her mother. I was sure that many women here did not even know where they were heading and what they were expected to do. Me and about five other ayahs were the only ones who seemed marginally level-headed.

Five months of cramped conditions, crying women and abysmal treatment soon would weave its way into my heart like firm thread slowly encasing the true me. I put up with my sorrow though.

THE MOMENT I stepped off that boat and onto solid ground was one of the best days of my life. Although, I was expecting the smell of sandalwood, marigold flowers and cooking turmeric and instead I was met with the odour of wet earth and bitter fumes which I soon began to choke on. Once I had stepped onto British soil I was guided to the house where I would be taking care of a child. Six-month-old baby Joseph Marshall. He had gorgeous blue eyes and glorious, bright strands of blond hair which had started to stick out from his scalp like needles.

No matter how hard I tried I couldn't pronounce his name though.

'Jo-seph,' Mrs Marshall would say.

'Do-sif,' I would reply, frustrated in myself.

Mrs Marshall then would get up, roll her eyes, walk out the door with her husband and not come back for the next couple of weeks or so. You see, I was the one who really took care of my darling boy Joseph. I tended to his leg when he fell down in the garden and scolded him when he stole food from the kitchen. I raised that boy to be a splendid young man. The language barrier was barely anything by the time he was two or so. We didn't need words to communicate that much anyway. I used my eyes, facial expressions, and gestures and even when Mr or Mrs Marshall hurled insults at me and called me a 'brown pig' Joseph would always come to my bed and wipe away the tears from my face as I held him close to my chest. He was the one sole thing that I truly cared for in that hell of a house. I put up with the rest of my sorrow.

WHEN JOSEPH TURNED seven my purpose at the Marshall house was no more. I didn't get to say goodbye to my blond-haired beauty and in a matter of hours Mr Marshall had ushered me out of the house and chucked a messily packed bag of my belongings at my feet.

'You stupid animal,' he mumbled as he shut the door once and for all.

So this is what I get for years of taking care of your son. Nursing him. Feeding him. Wiping his tears away while you waltz around at your parties and meetings.

I staggered across the street, nowhere to go and as useless as can be. The sorrow weighed heavy in my heart, but I put up with it.

44

FORGOTTEN DAYS

BY REGINA CORDERO

L ife Entry 845. August 21, 1975.

It was a sombre afternoon with the sunset saying it's last good-byes. The first year of law was starting. No more high school, no more easy assignments, no more old faces to greet. Boxes were piled across the new dorm like a horde of bulls came to mock my day even further. It was just not long when the letter came, right before the start of college. It was spotted with wet dots in its smooth envelope. It was from my best friend's mother:

"Dearest Abby. I feel terrible for pouring the news out with notes. Unfortunately, in my current position it's not possible. Fiona passed away this morning at early dawn. Her heart cancer is too much for my daughter to fight. Once again I'm sorry for not telling you with words."

Me and Fiona have been together since pre-school. Our parents would often buy us comics to read as we pretend to become the superheroes defeating the villains. It felt nothing could stop us between our bond. Sadly, I was wrong. The letter came with a package with a ripped note taped on the top. "Here is a box filled with memories when you were young. I hope you cherish them well with you." Inside were many different treasures that are worth more than jewels. There was our first craft we did with recycled bottles. We made a small castle with little figures where we played battle. There was small, wrinkled art with colourful silhouettes that I'm guessing is us. At the bottom of everything were carefully preserved letters that date back to grade 1. I started unfolding them carefully minding the delicate rips. One of them was the first message she ever sent by paper:

"Hi Abby! I saw you by the tree looking a bit lonely. Do you want to be my friend? My mother bakes her special cookies with a secret recipe that makes it taste like wonderland! See you in school tomorrow! Your fluffy mushroom, Fiona."

It gave me flashbacks all the way seeing a small girl staring at me by the swing eating a pink cookie. It made my heart glow with a warming peace. I decided to search deeper in the pile.

I found one at the day before our field trip:

"Hey Abby! My mother exchanged letters and decided you can stay the night over in my house! Bring some plastic bottles from the school project, maybe we can make something magnificent! Your only friend, Fiona. P.S.- We can stay the whole night reading comics if you want. Wink, wink."

I looked back at the old, brown bottles that were once clear and white. I decided to wash them and place them on my shelf later. I decided to read one more before dinner, for I have a celebratory dinner with my family for my graduation. If cancer could have waited another day then Fiona could be with hers. I found a clear white envelope with a unicorn sticker as its closure. "It can't be from when we were kids." I said to myself. "It would be mouldy and wrinkled by now."

"Dearest Abby. If you're reading this, I'm dead. I'm writing this a week before our- your college days begin. Please don't ever lose hope. I may not be your roommate, but I'm still your friend, am I not? I only have one wish to tell before I fade, don't ever stop being a hero. Become the lawyer you are now. You always have been my hero. Don't ever blame yourself, okay? Your fluffiest mushroom and only friend, Fiona. P.S.- I still believe Iron Man is the best."

I laughed at her last words to me. Not a mockery, but a sweet tender laugh, when she used to make jokes back in the old days. I'm making your wish come true Abby, I promise on mushrooms. There was only one thing that she was wrong about, she is *my* hero. But I still believe Captain America dominates all.

45

PEOPLE OF EVE

BY GRACE HOWELL

I t was a very long time ago, perhaps too long. We hear (and we could be wrong) that it was a time when there was peace-peace both in the place, and in the mind within the place.

Standing majestically in the centre of a Garden, proudly displaying delicate ruby red bulbs of delight, casting its own umbrella of shadow, was the Tree of the Knowledge of Good and Evil. And there (conveniently for its purposes) in the shadows, out of sight of the heaven above the clouds, was the living embodiment of malice and greed- the snake.

Craftily it wrapped itself, firmly, around the minds of two creatures, strangling their resistance to materialism, and squeezed out of them their downfall.

So Eve, a decisive girl (and we always get the blame for everything), grabbed the apple: she plucked a ruby delight from the tree. This version of the story can't be changed, for it is written, but the other versions of the story can be. However, today, the snake has remained with us.

The snake has shed and evolved to become money.

It can still wrap you up, because of its powerful body, made of coins and the green that glistens, that some people think are unreal in in what they call the virtual world – until, that is, they kill you, and you realise those muscles weren't virtual at all. And The Garden, of course, is fast becoming a dilapidated wreck, as we latch, grasp and snatch at any of the apples on the dying tree.

Our story of The Garden, like any story, can be changed, if the always accused Eve, and poor old 'She made me do it!' Adam, wake up to the boundless possibilities of what we can achieve when altruistic, compassionate and selfless. Some are already learning to be like that; the behind the scenes workers of the earth, the type of people who read this, just as you do, and realise they are one of Them.

Instantly, people think of those on the news, in the iridescent colours of the flag of the earth, green and blue, bellowing for the earth's rights. Most people haven't heard about Them, who actively fight for The Garden (not using 'ours' as it doesn't belong to us).

Maybe someone should bring their small acts into the spotlight, creating platforms where people share their stories of hope like a newspaper, social media page, a website... Though I barely know a single person who fits in this group, I know that, like a samizdat network, they are out there, writing the story again. Perhaps it goes like this....

.....having its muscles, but no voice to whisper in Eve's ear, the bored snake slithered off into a different, more snake-friendly story. In this story here, plucking the apple, Eve and Adam ate it, the juice spilling from their mouths, like teardrops, whilst the tree cried empty, silent screams, reminded of its loneliness. Gingerly, Eve and Adam extracted the core of the apple's life.

Then, naturally, they replanted it.

Every day they watered and nourished the little buds of life, to bring back the life they had borrowed. Soon, the next tree grew, then the next. The trees, and Eve, and Adam, and the people....they all bathed in the sunlight, and they all reached up, for something they hadn't found yet- a kind of peace of mind they'd heard of....

.......So Eve and Adam's kids (well, great-great-great-grand-etc kids; well, you) moved to an eco-friendly apartment in New York City (they didn't bring the snake), where Eve has a problem. Her psychiatrist friend

says it's just obsessive behaviour, but Eve (and Adam, who's an ecology-conscious politician) just freak out when they watch water fill up a bath. Weird, eh? In Eve's reflection in the reflections from the bath, there are people, whose throats crave just one drop, and the earth where the water cracks from breaking, like wrinkles in our skin. A fat old man on the TV, whose great-grandchildren might need to develop fin and scales to survive, think people like Eve are weird, people who put the earth first. Eve's psychiatrist friend asked about drugs, but Eve doesn't do drugs. Though her mother believes she is a saint, Eve knows she isn't; saints often overfill the bath.

Meanwhile, the fat old man on TV dreams of his holiday on a luxury island, where his pet snake, loose in house, is no problem. It would never harm his children....

46

THE EVERGREEN TREE

BY HANNAH CHO

Trembling, the woman held her child up to the dim light of the morning hours. After scrutinizing the newborn's healthy sheen, the new mother decided she would be named Ho Shim, meaning "generous heart". Born in 1939 in northern Korea, Ho Shim was the second of eight children.

There was only enough money for Ho Shim to study. So, Ho Shim studied, learning and growing faster than the barley shoots in the fields she romped about in. In elementary school, she read the novel Sangnoksu ("The Evergreen Tree") by author Sim Hun. She idolized the female protagonist, who strived to educate impoverished communities during Japanese occupation. Ho Shim also wanted to keep the culture and language of her country alive, amidst a time when Japan mercilessly tried to erase it all. And soon, the barley shoot dreamt of becoming a towering evergreen tree.

Even young Ho Shim knew tensions were high as Japan continued to infringe on Korea's arable rural land. For now, she diligently took care of her six younger siblings while dreaming of teaching the rest of her village. But the end of Japanese occupation in 1945 only marked the start of worse things that would topple Ho Shim's sheltered life.

. . .

Soon, with Korea on the verge of war, it was unsafe to stay in the North. 10-year-old Ho Shim left for the south with the remaining siblings who had survived thus far. Carrying the youngest on her back, Ho Shim walked until standing still to take a break felt disorienting. Her dream of becoming a countryside activist was no more but walking across Korea showed her the war-afflicted people who needed help.

Now in southern Korea, Ho Shim had an aching back but was safe. Even though continuing

education would be nonsensical to others, she completed middle school. This time, she

envisioned "working hard, living hard", and becoming a teacher for all, not just the countryside. She escalated to high school, then to the best women's college in Korea. Most girls her age were married with multiple children, but Ho Shim refused- she was going to get her teaching certification. Before she started working as a teacher, she decided to work as a curator at Changdeokgung Palace. Although it was almost completely destroyed during the Japanese occupation during Ho Shim's childhood, it was rebuilt from the ashes. Ho Shim felt it was a symbol of patriotic resilience, and to do her part for it, she curated the artifacts left behind by ancient royals - clothes, utensils, and diaries.

However, her back pain had started catching up to her big dreams. So, when her palace co-worker introduced her to Jong Sam Cho, Ho Shim decided she would finally get married. Afterall, her marriage could resemble that of the lovers in her favourite book, fellow activists who worked together to bring knowledge to all. But unfortunately, Ho Shim's husband was not nearly the educator she was. Jong Sam was an architect and had to travel often for construction projects. Ho Shim quickly found that she could no longer pursue being a teacher, as she had to spend all day taking care of her children while her husband was on work trips.

As TIME PASSED, Ho Shim spent her prime as a mother. Although her teaching credential was
never used, she continued to dream of keeping her culture alive. She steadily kindled her dream by teaching her children everything she knew, and eventually sent them off to the best colleges in Korea.

With her children now adults, an elderly Ho Shim had the time to fulfill her dreams. To get back on her path, Ho Shim did what she did best: learn. With vigour, she mastered classes on almost every topic, including an ancient royal culinary class.

ALTHOUGH THE ACUTE back pain from her arduous journey has long caught up, Ho Shim remains
sprightly thanks to her everlasting dream. Even now, Ho Shim volunteers to teach young children Korean culture and language, just as she taught me as a child.

Ho Shim is my grandmother and my hero. She has bestowed her story and ambition to her
children and grandchildren, and out of respect to her and my country, I keep my Korean heritage alive within my writing. Even now, it speaks to you and has bequeathed Ho Shim's spirit of resilience and passion that has continued to remain aflame for 83 years. May the spirit continue to burn within you and I to spread meaning, drive, and love through writing.

47

RIGHT TO LOVE

BY CAS CRUZ

Some say you don't ever forget your first love. I agree. Betty Doyle was my first love. Even though tons of years have passed, I still remember the feeling of her. Her essence. Her presence. She was everything to me. She was perfect. For a while, she was mine.

Betty and I grew up in a time where we couldn't exist. We were seventeen when things began to change. I still remember the day, laying on the floor of her tiny apartment on the upper east side. We were next to each other, and nothing else felt like it mattered.

"Etta," she whispered to me, her gentle hands combing through my hair. My name is Julietta Fletcher. She called me Etta, and every time she did it was music to my ears. "You know you have to leave before my pa comes home."

"Why?" I asked her, turning on my side so I could face her. "Can't two friends hang out in one's lounge?"

"He'll get suspicious of us. I can't risk that, Etta. I can't risk losing you."

The smile that once shone on my face twisted into a frown. Betty squeezed my hand.

"We've been over this, Et. We hang out after school, we go out as friends, but every other time it has to be in secret. No one can know about us. The real us, what we do when no one else is watching."

I rolled onto my back, brushing my hand over her carpet.

"I don't want who I am to be a secret," I admitted.

"I know, but I don't want anything to happen to you. To us, to what we have. Let's just enjoy being together- we only have a few minutes before you have to go."

And so, with music humming behind us, we continued to lay on the floor in the company of each other.

A few minutes before I had to leave, Betty decided to change the radio station. She was just flipping through them when we stopped on a news one. The voice on the radio was rambling on and on about the stonewall riots down in the village. My eyes lit up, and I quickly rose to my feet.

"Betty-" I began, walking over to her and grabbing her hand. "We should go. To the riots- we should fight, Betty, we should help-"

"Etta, you know I can't." Her voice was practically begging for me to just drop it. I knew she wanted to go, though. We both knew these protests were the first steps to change.

"School just got out a few days ago, the riots are livelier now than ever- we can go. We can go and then run away somewhere. These people are like us, Bet, they want the same thing we do."

A tear ran down her cheek. She shook her head, turning off the radio. "I can't. I'm sorry it's too risky- Et, my father will be home you should-"

"I should go," I finished her sentence for her. "I'm going down there. I'm gonna protest, I'm gonna fight for us. They can't keep me down Betty, they can't keep *us* down."

Tears now fell from both of our eyes.

"Be safe down there... I'll see you soon."

And then, I left.

I only stayed at the riots for a little while. The people there were fierce. We all wanted the same thing, though. We had a lot of rights, all but the right to love. That's what we wanted, but it was more than that. We wanted the right to be ourselves, ordinary people.

It's been over forty years. My bones are old and so is my soul, but my spirit is young and alive. We did win our rights. Thanks to the riots, I always believed those who protested at the Stonewall were sorts of heroes. They don't get enough recognition, not nearly as much as they deserve. Thanks to them, I now have the life I always wanted. Even if it did take decades to reach this point. It was all worth it.

Betty left a few weeks after the riots first broke out, because of her father. She moved upstate. I never saw her again, she never wrote. I think about her a lot, about the last time I saw her.

I wonder if she is living the life she always wanted, or if she is still stuck in the life everyone else wanted for her.

48

CONFLICTED HEARTS

BY AFINA LIANG

As a person who spends Friday nights binging shows, I often find myself admiring characters from books and TV shows. Fiction almost made me lose track of reality and realize there are real-life people around me that are just as interesting and brave. Recently, I confirmed that my brother is a hidden hero who is willing to sacrifice so much for the family. The realization was sudden, but the evidence had been right in front of me for years. A few years ago, my brother started to act as my guardian because of certain limitations my parents have. At first, I thought it was natural for him to take care of me since he is a capable adult. He would remind me to clean my room, take care of myself, and go to all the school events with me. However, I was confused about why he would offer help to my parents when he is so busy with work. So I asked.

He would always answer: "Because I love this family and my little sister."

It was later I realized he did not have the obligation to take care of me, yet he sacrificed his precious time to lecture and teach me. My big brother has always been a patient and caring person. It was a huge argument a while ago that forced me to look deeper into his character. An argument with him made me realize how I took so many things for granted and how lucky I truly am. One ordinary afternoon, my brother called me to clean my room, but I procrastinated. I did not know why that was a big deal and why he would care so much about my room. Perhaps out of laziness or rebellious personality, I ignored his command (like I've done many times before.) Then the next second, he shouted at me menacingly. The atmosphere was instantly tense, and his anger was palpable as he stormed down the stairs. I was completely shocked by his mood swings and unusual temper.

"All I want is what's good for you! Why can't you just listen to me..."

At that point, I felt as if he was guilt tripping me, so I said nonchalantly, "I know. I will do it later."

Then there was this terrible silence that lasted for centuries! When I turned my face, I saw droplets of tears on his cheek. It is so rare for him to cry so I instantly felt I'd done something horrible. I was acting like a leech that sucked out his patience while complaining about how he is not enough. I was scared of abandonment and full of self-resentment. My selfishness was exposed as if there was a gigantic mirror in front of me, finally reflecting my true nature. I hated my brother for his strict rules, and he knew that. Even so, he said he would rather let me hate him than abandon me. That was the transformative moment that felt like everything finally made sense. I noticed my brother's emotions and that he is a human too. If no one is giving him love and he always gives others love unconditionally, he will be drained one day. Instead of being absorbed in fiction, my brother's existence told me that there are many hidden aspects of a person that you can only reach by close observation and empathy. Heroes are not perfect, but they are people who are willing to sacrifice something to bring others happiness.

THROUGH APPRECIATING MY BROTHER, I also understood that every family member needs to take on certain responsibilities, so the family stays together. I don't exactly agree with my brother on many

49

AIRDOG GUNNER

BY CHARLOTTE LEE

"Sir, I can't lend your dog assistance for its broken leg without a name and serial number. Unless you're in place to give serial numbers for units, I'm afraid I cannot do anything." The airman glared at the nurse while holding the shaking Kelpie.

"Ma'am, call me Percy. I'm a Leading Aircraftman for WW2, and state that he'll be known as Gunner 0000. I ask for a repaired leg." The nurse reluctantly took Gunner and placed him on the ragged bed.

"Just know that this thing won't contribute to WW2, and only distract the Air Force." the crude nurse said.

"I found Gunner under a destroyed mess hut, whimpering with fear in his eyes. Seeing him desperately trying to get away from me, I knew the Japanese Air Force must have made him witness a terrible bombing. He'll know what's best for us after that experience." Percy held Gunner with care after the procedure, making sure not to tamper with his plastered leg. As Percy walked away from the field hospital, he reflected on what the nurse had said, but shook it off by talking to Gunner.

"Don't listen to that nurse because it sounded like she was brain-washed by a Nazi. We're headed to the airfield to repair some items.

Ever since the Japanese started attacking us for resources, our aircraft has been severely damaged." Approaching the airland, Percy was greeted with roars from the Chief of the Air Force.

"Percy! CAC Wackett's engine is busted and requires fixing immediately. Don't be late again or you'll face removal."

"Yes, sir!" Percy frantically yelled. As he placed Gunner in a safe range from the war aircraft, he reached his arm out to pet his head. Gunner scowled at Percy, thinking he'd attack him like the Japanese soldiers did. Percy backed off and ran to the aircraft before he heard the Chief's shouts again. As Percy was carefully installing a starter in the engine, Gunner suddenly became agitated, starting to jump and bark. The chief and other Air Force personnel looked at the anxious dog questionably. Percy ran to Gunner, attempting to shush him. Even though he had an injured leg, it seemed like he was in distress, trying to grab attention. Before the chief could yell at Percy, Japanese raiders began strafing the area. Everyone started scattering for shelter. Minutes after the attack, the airmen were commanded to head back to base for rest, making reconstruction delayed for tomorrow. Walking to the base, Percy simply let out, "Gunner?"

The following morning, Gunner began to whine and growl. Not long after, strafing happened in the Darwin Air Force Base, causing more destruction. The same patterns kept occurring with Gunner as weeks passed by, with the Australian Air Force lacking anticipation of incoming attacks.

Percy approached the chief with an anxious face, asking, "Chief, it's been a month since we were fully prepared for Japanese strafing since our radar picks up unknown aircraft slower than Gunner does. I should confront Wing Commander McFarlane for approval of Gunner becoming an alert for enemies." The chief was sceptical, but allowed Percy to ask. As Percy entered McFarlane's office while holding Gunner to his arms, he took a deep breath and discussed his idea.

"Gunner 0000 has accurate hearing that can detect enemy planes 20 minutes before our radar can, sir. I think it would be a great opportunity if you considered him an alarm."

McFarlane pondered on the idea. He came to a conclusion: "I'll announce to the Air Force to trigger the raid sirens when Gunner alerts them." Percy had a grin on his face. Once exiting the office, Percy quickly went to the airfield to do practice procedures. Gunner abruptly began barking, soon making raid sirens sound.

"Begin formation! Airmen assemble in planes and approach enemy aircraft! Surround as many enemies as possible!" the chief called out. Percy along with others jumped into their planes as they set off to attack. Japanese planes started to viciously bomb surrounding aircraft, while the Australian planes swiftly dodged each missile that passed by. The air was a cloud of smoke that made the area hardly visible to see. Percy had begun a dogfight on the last enemy plane that had run out of explosives, eventually making them retreat.

Returning to airland, Wing Commander McFarlane stepped in front of Gunner and Percy.

"Gunner 0000, you're always welcomed to the Australian Air Force for your responsibility and dignity. You'll be considered our Airdog Hero."

50

ILE OMINIRA: HOME OF FREEDOM

BY OLUNIMI SONOWO

L*ori oke o'un petele* (On the top of the hill)
   Ibe l'agbe bi mi o (That was where I was born)
   Ibe l'agbe to mi d'agba oo (That is where I grew up) *Ile ominira* (Home of Freedom)

My grandmother would hum these words as she hobbled around the house. When I was younger, I would often sway to the beat of her melodious voice, trying to mimic her words, words that were meant to be spoken with ease, but were completely alien to me.

"We are a people of pride, of great talents and rich culture. We shall not be dominated," my grandmother would often say. 'We' was referring to the Egba people of Abeokuta in Ogun State. "The Egba people, the descendants of the opulent Oyo Empire and founders of Abeokuta, the Egba people, a people to envy." She would often boast. Alas, when I thought of the Egba people, I thought of bad roads, stained with red clay dirt and dust. I saw no reason why the Egba people of Abeokuta should be envied, why my people were so special.

My great-grandmother, Kikelomo, lived during a time when the Egba people were oppressed and held by an iron fist. She witnessed her mother struggle to pay her taxes. Her mother, sisters and herself would be at the market stall at dawn and leave at dusk. Despite the effort made by her and many women in her community, they still laboured vigorously to pay these taxes they were subjected to.

"Join the Abeokuta women's union for the freedom of Egba women." My great-grandmother would often hear these calls in the market. She had considered joining the union, but after her husband's stern warning against it she relented, or so her husband thought. "Mama still snuck out to the secret meetings. It was enlivening to feel hope again." My grandmother would say as she talked of her childhood.

It was finally the year 1946. The Alake of Egbaland had increased the flat-rate tax on women. It was then that the AWU began their mass protests, involving marching outside the king's palace and demanding the abolishment of direct taxation. My great-grand-mother was only twenty-seven years old when she lost her life during the Massacre of 1946 - when the colonial authorities released tear gas and beat women up during a protest in October, 1946.

My family was never the same. My grandmother became a very active member in the AWU, attending meetings and rallying women together. Finally in the year 1949, the Alake of Egbaland was over-thrown and the taxes were abolished. While the victories had been great, some losses had been greater.

The Egba women of Abeokuta remain the unsung heroes of female liberation, female rights protection, and ultimately female freedom. So, when I am asked where I'm from on cultural days, I wear my iro, buba and gele with pride and say, "My name is Oluwalonimi and I am a proud Egba woman!"

51

CHILD SOLDIERS IN THE KOREAN WAR

BY SOFIA FORBES

For teens and kids like me, school and chores are the only things we need worry about. Not many of us have to constantly wonder if we have to kill someone to prevent ourselves from being killed. We can get an education and grow up, never having to worry about getting kidnapped from our homes and being forced into the army. This isn't the case for tens of thousands of children. A lot of people know about child soldiers, particularly because in places such as Africa, some places in South America, and the Middle East these children are forcibly used for war or other inhumane violations.

Many of these children and teens have been coerced into becoming soldiers or slaves and even when they were given a choice, their options are usually join or die. They're forced to witness and commit horrific acts of violence against people - including their own family and friends - or otherwise face torture and/or murder. These kids aren't physically ready for war but it's obvious that the leaders who use child soldiers don't care. They enlist children to fight and don't even bother to think about the consequences. Just like adult soldiers, children who are forced to fight in war also suffer from

PTSD or other psychological and physical disorders. Without the right type of support, it would be harder to cope with the disorders.

In the Korean Conflict - a proxy war that not many people know about - both South and North Korea enlisted children to fight during the war. 3,000 of the 30,000 total children died during the conflict. Many were forced to become soldiers against their will much like the modern-day child soldiers. Another similarity between both modern-day child soldiers and the ones in the Korean War was that they were underfed. This made it harder to have the energy to carry the heavy equipment most soldiers are given as well as participate in the long treks across usually rough terrain. Some of these soldiers have had to kill their comrades or commit other acts of violence which could elicit PTSD, depression, or other trauma related disorders. For most people, it's hard to talk about traumatic events because reliving something that caused a person physical or emotional pain is a difficult thing to do.

Life after the war for the South Korean child soldiers was still rough. Some of the soldiers had multiple jobs and many of them couldn't finish their education. While North Korea dedicated a monument to their child soldiers who fought during the war, South Korea refused to acknowledge the children who sacrificed their childhood and on occasion - their lives. I believe it's wrong that the government tried to almost erase the fact that they used child soldiers during the war. The former child soldiers asked the South Korean government

to create a memorial that was dedicated to the children who sacrificed their lives. After so many years of being ignored, however, many of them got discouraged.

Creating a memorial for the child soldiers during the Korean War will help remind South Korea as well as the world, about what happens when child soldiers are used in war rather than glorifying it the way North Korea did. If South Korea doesn't acknowledge the former child soldiers, they could end up repeating that mistake in a future war.

Children should be able to grow up feeling safe and well cared for. They shouldn't have to worry about getting murdered or tortured or having to commit those acts. The warring African, South American, and Asian governments need to stop using child soldiers and find a way to protect the kids who are kidnapped. Protecting citizens and children is an important part of ruling a country. It's frustrating to think that these governments aren't enforcing the laws stopping children from being forced into the military and slavery. We can't change the fact that child soldiers were used in the Korean Conflict and modern wars, but we need to remember their sacrifices and stop using child soldiers in wars.

Some people may ask why we should learn about the Korean child soldiers. I believe it's important because not many people talk about the Korean Conflict. If we exclude the children who fought in the war, people will never know all the sacrifices that were made during the war.

52

THE LINES OF SKIRTS

BY PATRICIA ZHANG

T he picket lines were lined with dirt and valour. Dust flew into the eyes of the protesting workers. Sweat stuck to their faces and ran down their necks. They gritted their teeth and continued. This had to be done, the conditions in the mines were unbearable. On top of that, the pay was discriminatory and unfair. One way or another, change had to be made.

Of the participants, men were the overwhelming majority, yet unseen allies helped the cause in the households. They went beyond packing meals and cleaning clothing. From the back lines to the front, the miners' wives became a fortuitous resource to help the strike, yet their actions remain unsung today.

New Mexico was a mining hotspot, and the town dubbed "Zinc Town" was home for many miners and their wives. These women had roles; cook, cleaner, caretaker. They dragged through days and bore the blunders of rudimentary daily tasks. Their knuckles red from scrubbing, faces worn out by long days. Yet when the strike began, they quickly found themselves in a new scenario, which would result in an unconventional tale of women's solidarity.

The Mexican miners had been working day in and out, but whispers of discriminatory and immoral pay spread like a disease. This led to the fateful day of October 17, 1950, when the Empire Zinc strike began. It seemed inevitable but it required staggering amounts of courage from the miners and their families. Also dubbed the Salt of the Earth strike, miners refused to work and turned to picketing. They laid down their pickaxes and raised their voices, demanding for change.

However, their employer, Empire Zinc, struck back hard and fast. Empire Zinc could pressure the workers back into doing their jobs, and they would

be baked right into silence once again. Yet this was when the heroes of the story came to light.

The women became the pickerters. It was a radical movement. It was revolutionary. Women went from supporting the picketers to being the picketers themselves. From the bases to the front

lines. In a way that changed the narrative of these women's lives forever, they began to start picketing. Displaying flagrant fearlessness and resolve, they became the new face of the movement. Policies that stopped the men from participating in unionization didn't apply to the women who didn't officially work for Empire Zinc. This immunity became the key to women leading the protest.

As their demands were formally rejected and laughed off by men, now they were accepted. They were appreciated, realized for their actual value and importance. Previous requests that were laughed at now had significance once the men at home began to realize just how essential the women's work was. When women took their places at the picket lines, the men shifted to the households and found out the womens demands were valid. Their voices were now heard, a wave of advocacy that was both unpredicted and important. There was now a newfound respect for these women who bore their heads through tough times and now were marching for reform. A more united front was born, with women leading the way forward.

The conditions pushing against the Mexican miners and their wives were being pushed back with the strike. The result? An act was one of not only miners' rights but a tale of determination of the miners' wives. With bravery thought by men as impossible for a woman to possess, they continued the advocacy for change. They created a new tale, one of pushing for the right thing, no matter how long and how painful. The women stood up to Empire Zinc without regrets or hesitation. No doubt, the strike would have ended sooner than its famous 15-month period if only the women didn't stand up.

But they stood and stuck together. They pushed and prodded and kept their heads high. A true act of defiant courage. They were important back then and they should be as important today. Heroes that pushed for innovation. Heroes not because they outmuscled their opponents, but because they persevered.

53

THE MOUNTAIN

BY ZIXUAN WANG

Every morning, fog surrounds the mountain. A few sparrows ring out in the forest, and a dog barks as if to express the vitality of this land. The sky is slightly illuminated. In a small, open space in the middle of the mountains, there are only a few families who get up very early. They seem to have begun a busy day. In the faint morning light, a faltering old man carries a large basket--this morning's picked corn. His limping gives away the fact that the old man's physical strength has been eroded by the years. What makes an old man in his seventies get up so early?

A car is parked at the intersection of the village. Loudly slamming the door, a man in a suit and sunglasses and a young boy with fancy headphones and a mobile device in-hand exit the car. The city-bred teenager is rebellious and lawless. Today's rapid development of the Internet has made him addicted to clearing customs in games and posting on social networks. This makes the teenager frivolous and impervious to the feelings of others. After another quarrel with his parents, the teenager was sent to a place he had never thought of.

Now, looking at the grandfather, the teenager is a little overwhelmed: he sees the dirt on his grandfather's clothes and the shoes that have long been worn out. The yellow dog rushes up and rubs against him, and the boy has a disgusted expression on his face. Maybe it was out of politeness, maybe it was the nervousness of seeing him for the first time, but the young man whispers, "Hello, Grandpa."

The first time the boy enters his grandpa's house, he sees the bed, table, and floor full of dirt. The grandpa says in a strong accent, "Boy, don't stand there. Go rest for a while. You must be tired after driving for so long." The grandpa's caring greetings made the boy's scolding. The boy opened his mouth and didn't know what to say, so he took his clothes and left. This was the first time that the sensitive heart of a teenager had been illuminated by the care of his grandfather.

The grandpa cared about the boy from the very first day, and every morning before dawn, he went to the fields to pick fresh vegetables to make breakfast for his grandson. Although the conditions in the mountains were not good, the grandpa would squat down and wipe the ground and table with a rag every day, and a simple smile always accompanies the question, "What do you want to eat today?" Companionship can change a lot. The old man is like a beam of light, which energizes and wakes up the boy. He didn't need sophisticated educational methods. It was just the daily company of grandpa and the changes in the environment that made the young man, who seemed to be polluted, become clear again--from a big vat of dye to clear water.

Throughout that summer, there seemed no end to time. In the morning, the teenager would go with his grandfather to fertilize the fields, feed the fish in the pond, and take care of the small farm animals raised by his grandfather. His favourite pastime was to adventure into the mountains with the big yellow dog. The two played every day until the sun went down. The teenager even became friends with the neighbour's children. Among these kids, you see no games, no impetuous social status, no strict discipline--all these teenagers are just that, teenagers. They love to play, try, and explore.

The personality changes of the youth are obvious and good. Flirty, immature problematic teenager in the beginning to the optimistic and cheerful boy now. There are many smiles on the face of the boy. The boy's body has grown stronger, and his complexion has been tanned by the sun. When the boy left, he hugged his village friends tightly, gave the dog its favourite bone, and looked at the rickety body of his grandfather. Tears came out for some unknown reason, so he rushed to hug the old man who changed his life immeasurably. The old man still had the same white clothes, the same broken shoes, and the same simple smile as the first time he saw him. He hugged his grandson, patted his back lightly, and said, "Child, you should go."

Even with muddy white clothes, worn shoes, and a hunched body, Grandpa is a kind, selfless, hero.

54

YOUR FOUNDATION

BY RYAN AL-TURK

I get up, rub my eyes, and start the day afresh, making my way over to the bathroom. Like anyone else, I shower and brush my teeth, neglecting to floss as I rush to get my clothes on and get out the door. I grab a brown paper bag with a lunch I packed last night and head to my car.

As I take the usual route to work, I curse my luck for having been stopped by a red light. Begrudgingly, I abide by the law and wait for the go-ahead, continuing my way to work when granted confirmation.

Eventually, I make my way to this month's site. Whilst smaller than past sites it still remains a difficult task, building from the ground up. So, I pick up my hardhat and hi-vis jacket and get to work.

Walking over to a half-complete wall, I notice the mortar and bricks laying nearby, strewn across the ground in an orderly manner with what you'd expect to find nearby: a trowel, level, and brick jointer. With these as my tools, I get to work, picking up a trowel, scooping up some mortar, and laying a brick.

Repeating this cycle across the wall, I eventually find myself having to move up a level, so I do. This happens multiple times and I find myself completely engrossed in my work. Before I can get too focussed, a voice shouts to me, serving as a reminder of lunch.

I walk over to my car, picking up my lunch and sitting around with my colleagues, discussing whatever comes to mind as we take this time to relax. As per usual, we eventually reach the end of our break and return to our work, little changing other than our progress.

As the clock strikes 5, we finish up and make our way home, another hard day's work completed.

I get home, welcomed by my wife and child. We talk about how our days were over dinner, tales far more riveting than my own revealed to me as I learn more about the day's ins and outs.

Having finished dinner, we sit and talk more as we watch something on the TV. Eventually, time catches up to us and night crawls over us, so we put our kid to bed and find ourselves asleep as well.

This cycle repeats, day in, day out: I wake up, prepare for the day, lay bricks, come home and sleep.

My reward? I receive neither honour nor glory; I'm hardly recognised for my efforts past a paycheck. But there is one thing I receive: satisfaction.

Over time I get to marvel as we create something, anything, from the ground up, laying the foundations ourselves. Many times, these buildings come to be cherished by families like my own, no longer being just a hunk of bricks but becoming something more. A home.

Throughout history there have been people like me, laying bricks for a living, hardly recognised, hardly congratulated. We always finish the job though, through thick and thin we push ourselves through it, whether that be to provide for our families or another.

I may not have put the roof over your head, but someone like me did.

55

BROKEN YET WHOLE

BY ANDERS LEE

My mental health hasn't been the best lately. The algorithm knows that too. I get ads on social media for help lines, trauma therapy, and counselling. Most of the time, my thumb instinctively taps the screen; my brain doesn't want to know it's dysfunctional, rather, it seeks to live vicariously through snapshots of others. One ad caught my brain through. I hesitated and took a moment to process what was before my eyes. "When you have been traumatised, you ARE changed, but that does not mean you are less: like the *Kintsugi* bowl fixed with gold." A slew of meaningless hashtags followed, and I chuckled. I took a screenshot, with the intent to send it to my friends, but left the image sitting in my camera roll. That ad was enough to rewire my brain; surely #trauma would show up again and put me into a fit of laughter. So, each time I saw a mental health ad, I'd stop and analyse it closely. It wasn't long before another one popped onto my feed. This one was for a peer-to-peer community. I thought the ad had potential. Scouring for more funny information, I clicked the website.

My eyes started to water, my body froze, and my brain shut down —the exact opposite reaction of what I hoped for. Instead of promoting useless ways of alleviating trauma, the webpage included posts from real adolescents. There were no images or clever ways to boost engagement, though, just raw text and nothing more. I was crying because I was reading someone's story. Their post entitled, "when i die soon no one will care", was among the most recently published. The first line was an earnest introduction—Charly was 13-years-old. The next line, however, brought me to tears. "I wish I died when I OD [I] wish I took more I wish life wasn't so unfair." The rest of the story details Charly's life with depression, high expectations from parents, toxic relationships, anorexia, and a failed suicide attempt. It was written in such a manner to feel like a run-on sentence; every word you were gasping for air. That was enough to put my brain into perspective.

I felt obligated to post a response. I made an account and instantly started typing. I responded like I would to a friend—in lower-case. I wished Charly the best. Yet, when I pressed 'reply', it gave me a pop-up saying I'd have to wait for my comment to get moderated.

As MUCH AS we can complain that the system is working against youth with mental health issues, the invisible people within the system are working tirelessly. They are fostering an environment where youth feel comfortable enough to show their vulnerability. They are trying and they *are doing enough*. However, that doesn't make the mental health system exempt from criticism. Sometimes the people who need help are the ones helping. It much reflects the Japanese artform of *Kintsugi*. Perhaps we really are pieces of shattered pottery, glued back together with gold that glimmers eternally. We are broken, yet whole.

2021 12-16 CATEGORY WINNER

GUEST STORY - UNTHEMED

56

TRAIN TRACKS

BY LENA KILLALEA

A na didn't like that she couldn't see past five feet in front of her. She didn't like that anything could be lurking in the sleeping undergrowth, and she'd have been none the wiser. She had resolved to simply not taking her eyes off the dark green mass that lay beyond the train tracks, as if the bushes would slowly unfurl before her if she commanded them to. She imagined them peeling back leaf by leaf to reveal a pulsing clump of darkness, pricked with fur and adorned with yellow eyes that saw everything Ana couldn't. Each swish of a tree branch and pull of a bush in the wind teased her, threatening to let her in, let it out.

It was only the sudden snap from behind her that broke her focus, stealing the little girl's breath with a yelp. She almost didn't turn around at all. *I don't need to,* she assured herself meekly. *I can already see you. I can see you, so you can't scare me.* Blood rushed to her head and her breath was yanked from her chest as she realised that she could not see where the snap came from, but she could hear it. Slow, low, growling breaths. Closer, closer. Closer, closer. She squeezed her eyes shut, hugging her knees to her chest. *I take it back, I take it all back.* She bit her lip, trying to keep a sob in. *I don't need to see you, please. I can't! I can't see you.* A flash of yellow flashed in the dark night, just beyond the reach of Ana's vision. Its glow grew closer, travelling further into her line of sight like a blinking lighthouse. She could feel tears pooling in her eyes. Ana only opened her eyes to crane her neck in the opposite direction, looking for any sign of life, any sign of her mother, late to pick her up.

She'd been sitting on the plain wooden bench for hours, watching the sun slip lower and the moon rise to glory. Long ago she'd come to the conclusion that her mother wasn't coming, and she'd simply have to wait for morning light to guide her home alone. But she didn't want the morning light to take her home now. She wanted her mother.

She slowly turned her head back to the train tracks, then to the undergrowth which had been so sure was hiding something, then the grassy fields that lay next to that, and then to her right. She didn't see any feet, paws, limbs of any sort, save for the rhythmic *crunch, crunch, crunch* of broken undergrowth. Something was there. It couldn't be her imagination anymore. Something stretched forward from the sound of the crunch, sparsely covered in thick, black fur being shoved back and forth by the gusts of wind. With every *swoosh* of the creature's fur, a deep, growling breath ran through the night. Ana bit her tongue and tried not to scream. She kept her gaze focused on the trees in front of her, which had become doubly more inviting in the past few minutes. But with every swoosh, breath and crunch, curiosity thrummed inside her. Like whatever was prowling beside her could be no worse than her imagination. The sounds continued, rhythmic and steady and losing their danger with every second. She let her gaze flick back.

Two empty yellow circles met her gaze, floating in black fur, tucked away inside sunken in eye sockets. Blood rushed to Ana's eyes, her eyes widened, and she was standing before she knew what she was doing. The creature seemed to be pulsing, gravitating to the spot right in front of her, only to be back at the edge of the train station as soon as Ana realised it had moved at all. She couldn't keep her eyes away from it. Or rather, away from its eyes. They were full of a great nothingness, pure yellow painting the inside of the globes completely. They called to her.

How long have you been here?

The question was struck in Ana's mind like a match, put there by something hoping to explode her brain. She didn't have an answer. She could think of nothing, not when the clump of matter that stood some feet away from her was staring bright yellow daggers into her eyes, as unpredictable as a gust of wind. Slowly, it turned, exposing a shrivelled spine, yellowed with age like the pages of a book, scarcely covered by fur. Every creak of a limb that shifted as it moved felt more grotesque than the last, revealing some hidden scar or clump of flesh that clung to the thing's bones. Ana felt bile pool up her mouth, scratching like rust as it mixed with the sobs in her throat. And yet, she moved. Like she was being called, beckoned by the dark array of limbs, she moved. The sound of her heart thrumming in her chest drowned out the noise of the leaves beneath her feet, and her vision was blurred with tears. Still, Ana followed.

I can't go back. I can't, I couldn't. She broke her gaze from the hunkering shape of the thing as it lumbered on heavily ahead of her, craning her neck toward the bench. It was desolate save for her quilt-covered bag that only she knew how to handle, the spot where she had sat now chillingly empty.

A small voice spoke out into the silence in her head. *Go now. You'll go mad if you don't follow him.* A chill crept down the girl's spine. Dread dripped slowly through her as she realised she had to turn around. She had to keep going, let the creature lure her to wherever it pleased, because there was nothing worse than not knowing. And Ana knew, deep in her heart, that she'd follow it to the edge of the world if it called to her. Something about those eyes. When she turned to face it, the thing had gotten closer, creeping nearer when her back was turned. *Making sure I can't leave,* Ana realised with a start. *Making sure I won't leave.* The creature didn't keep walking once Ana turned back though. It opened its mouth, fleshing dangling from near invisible lips and teeth sharpened to a point, on the verge of tipping from its mouth. No sound came out. No sound was needed to scare Ana stiff. Finally, when its mouth began to close, only then did it turn and walk. And like she was tied to a string, Ana followed.

The pebbles that scattered the train tracks pricked at the soles of her feet through her thin shoes, eyes focused on the lumbering mass of the creature ahead. If she forgot about its breathing, its slow, haunting breathing, she could almost calm down. But every breath, every creak of a limb only served as a reminder that the creature was alive, it was there a few feet in front of her and she was chained to it. Her mind belonged to the creature. Her mind belonged to fear, fear of what she might decide was true if she didn't know what was really true. She lost all sense of human pain as she walked. She felt herself grow older, but not wearier. Her feet didn't hurt from the harsh ground she walked on, she did not grow tired from travelling for so long without rest. She only felt the beat of her heart and the echo of her distant breath. A spiralling fear pushed her forward. Whatever Ana might see as she followed this creature to the depth of oblivion, she feared the inside of her mind more. The rattle of an approaching train faded into nothing, the song of a far-off world. The lights dancing from the driver's carriage didn't burn as brightly as the light of the creature's eyes burned into her brain. But none of that stopped the train, hurtling into the night as it always did.

Ana never found out where the creature was going.

Two maintenance officers found her the next morning. A tragedy, they said. Poor little girl, what could have happened? The trains were running as normal, they pointed out. Why was she on the tracks? There's nothing dangerous around these parts, they decided. The trees screamed through their leaves for the thousandth time. *Look*

ACKNOWLEDGMENTS

Thank you to my inspiring and encouraging wife, Becki, for her eternal support and encouragement with this project and every other. She helps me with good ideas as much as saving me from my, erm, less good ideas.

The competition would not have come to be without the help, guidance and advice of Jan Carr, Mark Hood, Lynne Clark, Adam Jarvis and Tara Marakat. Sometimes you need to hear when the front cover you designed is rubbish or be told "a nine year old couldn't have written that, it reads like Paradise Lost". They have all given their best to reading many, many stories, and provided valuable insights.

Julian Barr, our editor, has been fantastic, as noted by the young writers and judges. He strikes the right note and is a pleasure to work with.

Thank you Mark Stay and Mark Desvaux, who backed me to start this competition in 2021 without any real proof it would work out. A healthy fear that I might ruin their reputations spurred me on.

Thanks again to those who provided their writing tips for the young writers—Nadia L. King, H.D. Coulter, Mark Stay, Caimh

McDonell, Ian W. Sainsbury, Cristy Burne, Josh Langley, and all the judges.

Thank you to my parents for always supporting me, and to Gareth & San for providing advice and encouragement.

Thank you Maria and Olunimi for reading out your stories for the YouTube channel. They were moving, composed and inspiring.

Thank you Esther Li who donated her $100 prize money from the 2021 competition into this year's pot, and to Dharshwana for donating theirs to charity.

Thank you to Wags, our lovely dog who has sat by me whilst reading through many stories, filled in spread sheets and sent a million emails (all of which are probably too long). I should really re-write that to make it clear I was completing all those tasks, not Wags...

Thank you to all the people who helped with advertising: Denise Hill from NewPages.com, Christopher Fielden, Melinda Tognini, Fabostory.wordpress.com, Tom Tolkien from schoolreadinglist.com, and anyone else who spread the word.

Finally, thank you to every single young person who wrote an original story and trusted us with it. My biggest fear when I started the Writing Tournament was, "nobody is going to enter". People did enter, and I thought "it's all going to fall apart!" Well, thanks to everyone involved it didn't fall apart. Phew.

The stories and the kind emails have made all the effort worthwhile for everyone involved.

Thank you, as always, to anyone I've forgotten to thank, but who contributed in some way. I'll forever feel bad about it, I promise.

ABOUT THE AUTHOR

W.J. Kite is the author of upcoming young adult fiction inspired by the Border Reivers. In 2022 he turned his focus to non-fiction writing and politics to promote animal rights and veganism, but will continue with his fictional series, perhaps sharing George R.R. Martin's recent commitment to deadlines.

For more information on his writing or the Writing Tournament please head to www.wjkite.com.

www.ingramcontent.com/pod-product-compliance
Lightning Source LLC
Chambersburg PA
CBHW032211170626
46808CB00006B/2426